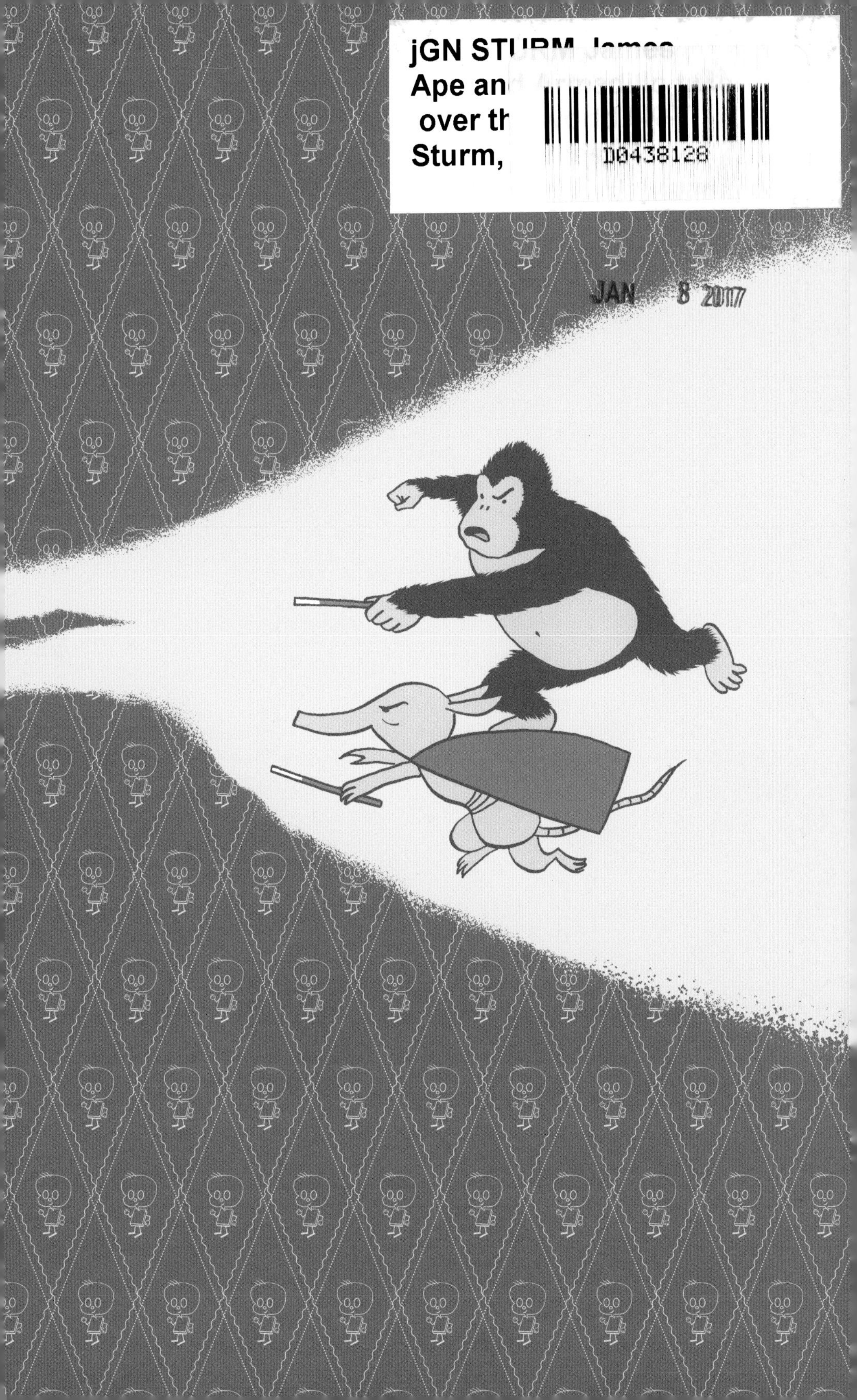

APE and ARMADILLO TAKE OVER the WORLD

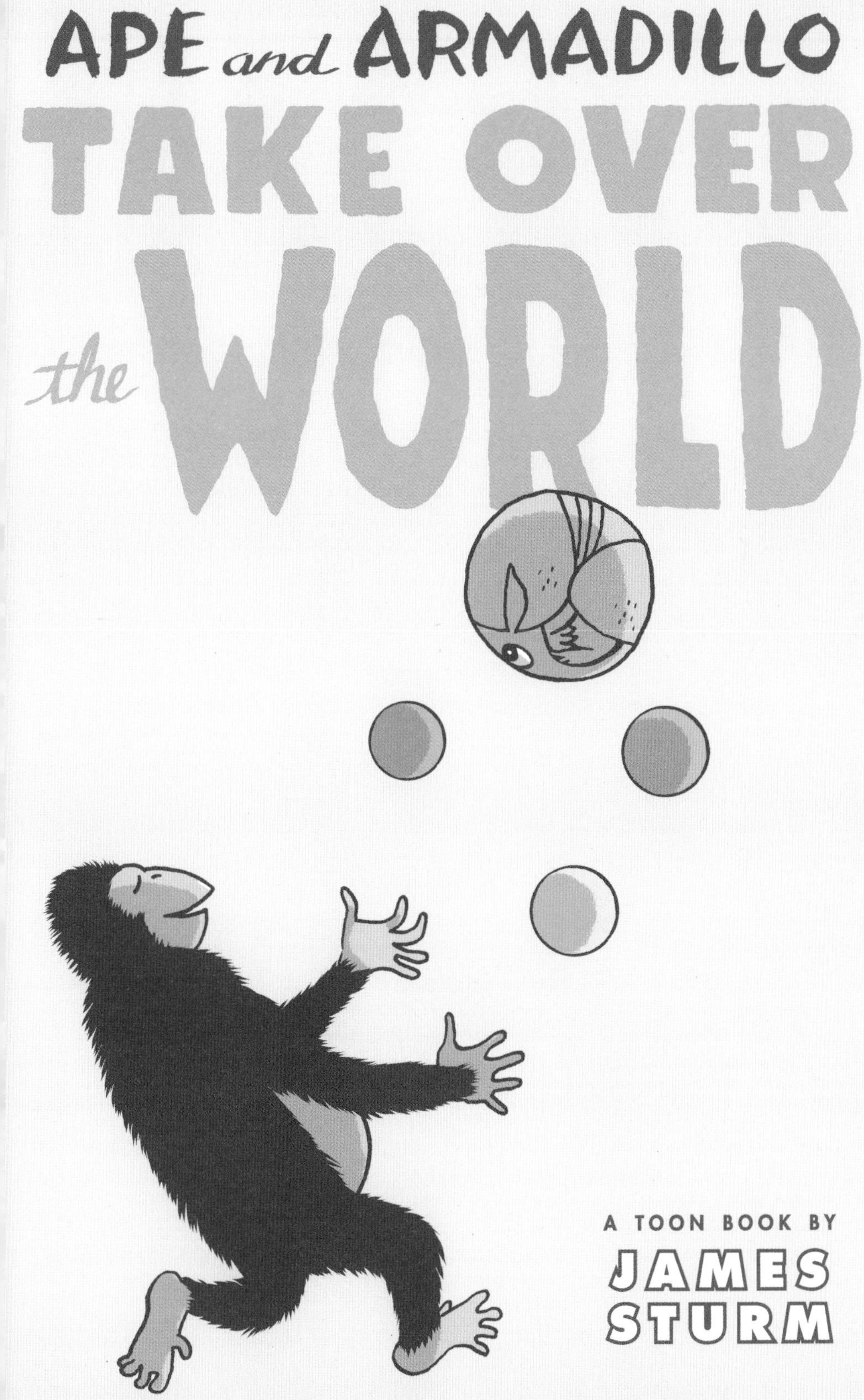

A TOON BOOK BY

JAMES STURM

A JUNIOR LIBRARY GUILD SELECTION

For Eva, Charlotte, & Rachel
(and the dogs, too)

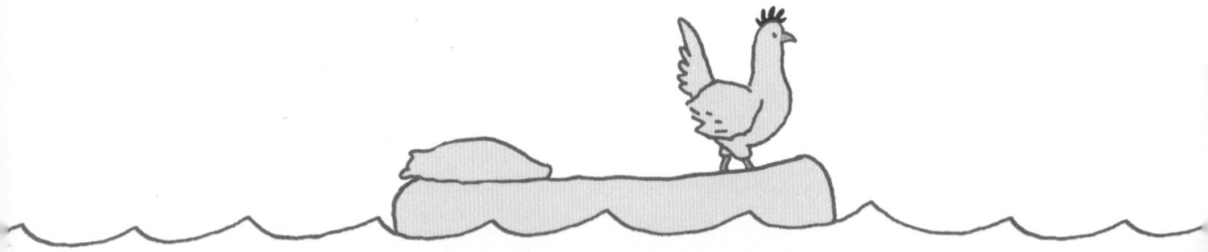

Editorial Director : FRANÇOISE MOULY

Design: JAMES STURM & FRANÇOISE MOULY

JAMES STURM'S artwork was drawn with brush and pen in India ink and colored digitally.

 All our books are Smyth Sewn (the highest library-quality binding available) and printed with soy-based inks on acid-free, woodfree paper harvested from responsible sources. Library of Congress Cataloging-in-Publication Data: Name: Sturm, James, 1965- author, illustrator. Title: Ape and Armadillo take over the world / by James Sturm. LCCN 2016003370 | ISBN 9781943145096 (hardback) Subjects: LCSH: Graphic novels. | CYAC: Graphic novels. | Friendship--Fiction. | Imagination--Fiction. | Apes--Fiction. | Armadillos--Fiction. | BISAC: JUVENILE FICTION / Comics & Graphic Novels / General. | JUVENILE FICTION / Imagination & Play. | JUVENILE FICTION / Action & Adventure / General. | JUVENILE FICTION / Readers / Intermediate. Classification: LCC PZ7.7.S84 Ape 2016 | DDC 741.5/973--dc23 Printed in China by C&C Offset Printing Co., Ltd. Distributed to the trade by Consortium Book Sales; orders (800) 283-3572; orderentry@perseusbooks.com; www.cbsd.com.

ISBN: 978-1-943145-09-6 (hardcover)

16 17 18 19 20 21 C&C 10 9 8 7 6 5 4 3 2 1

www.TOON-BOOKS.com

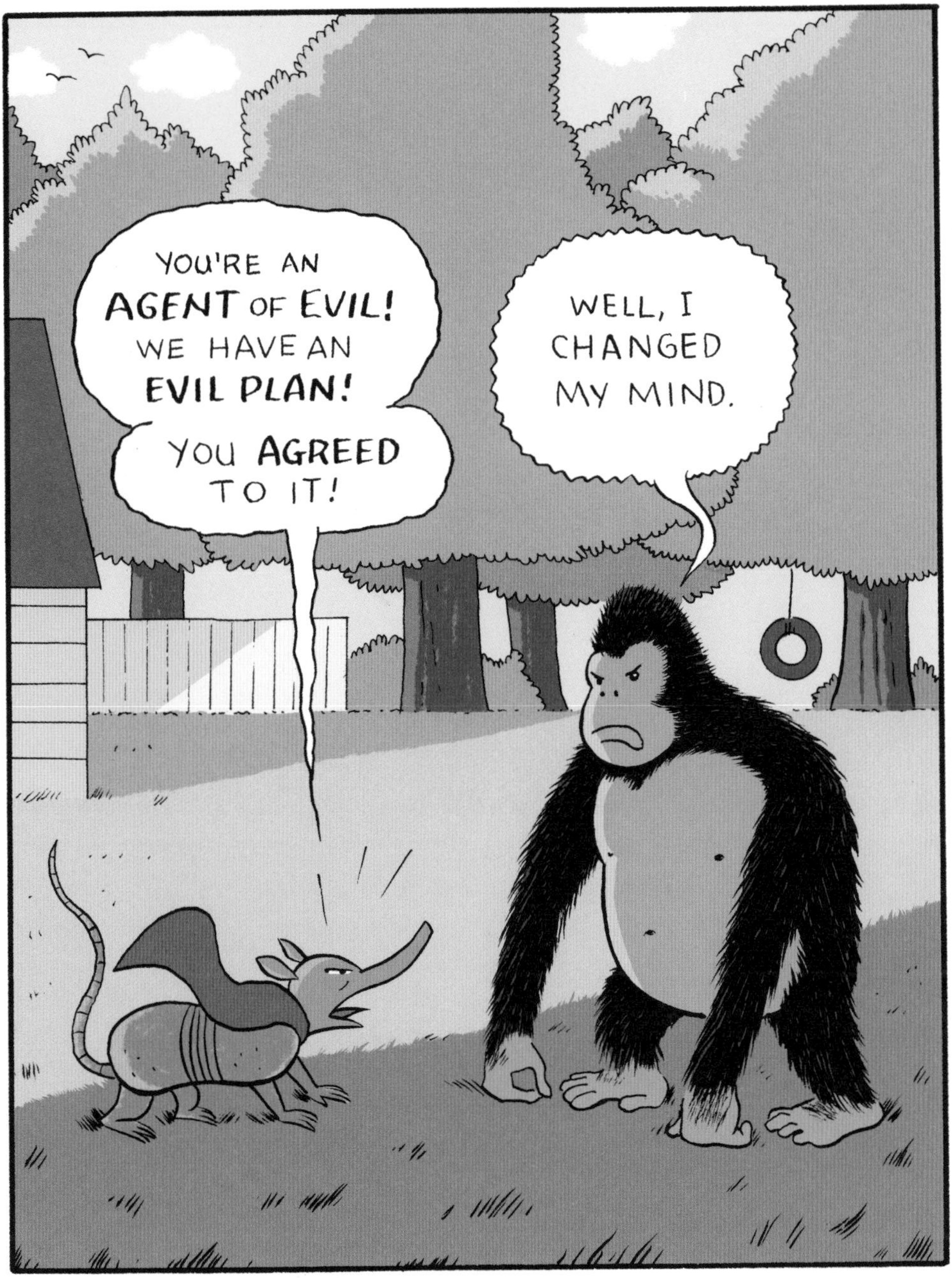
YOU'RE AN AGENT OF EVIL! WE HAVE AN EVIL PLAN!
YOU AGREED TO IT!
WELL, I CHANGED MY MIND.

BONUS COMICS

ARMADILLO AND HIS CAPE

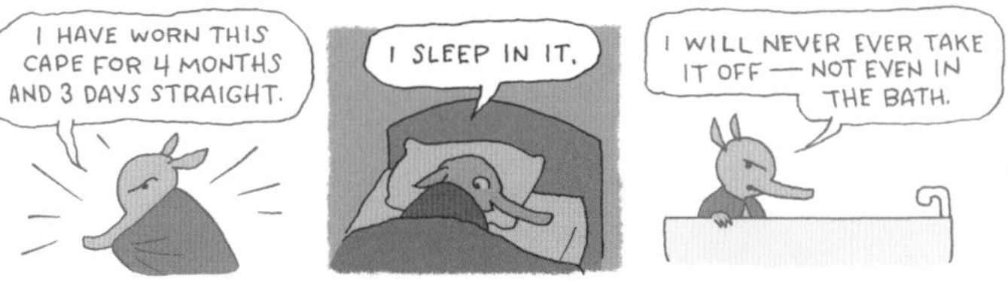
I HAVE WORN THIS CAPE FOR 4 MONTHS AND 3 DAYS STRAIGHT.
I SLEEP IN IT.
I WILL NEVER EVER TAKE IT OFF — NOT EVEN IN THE BATH.

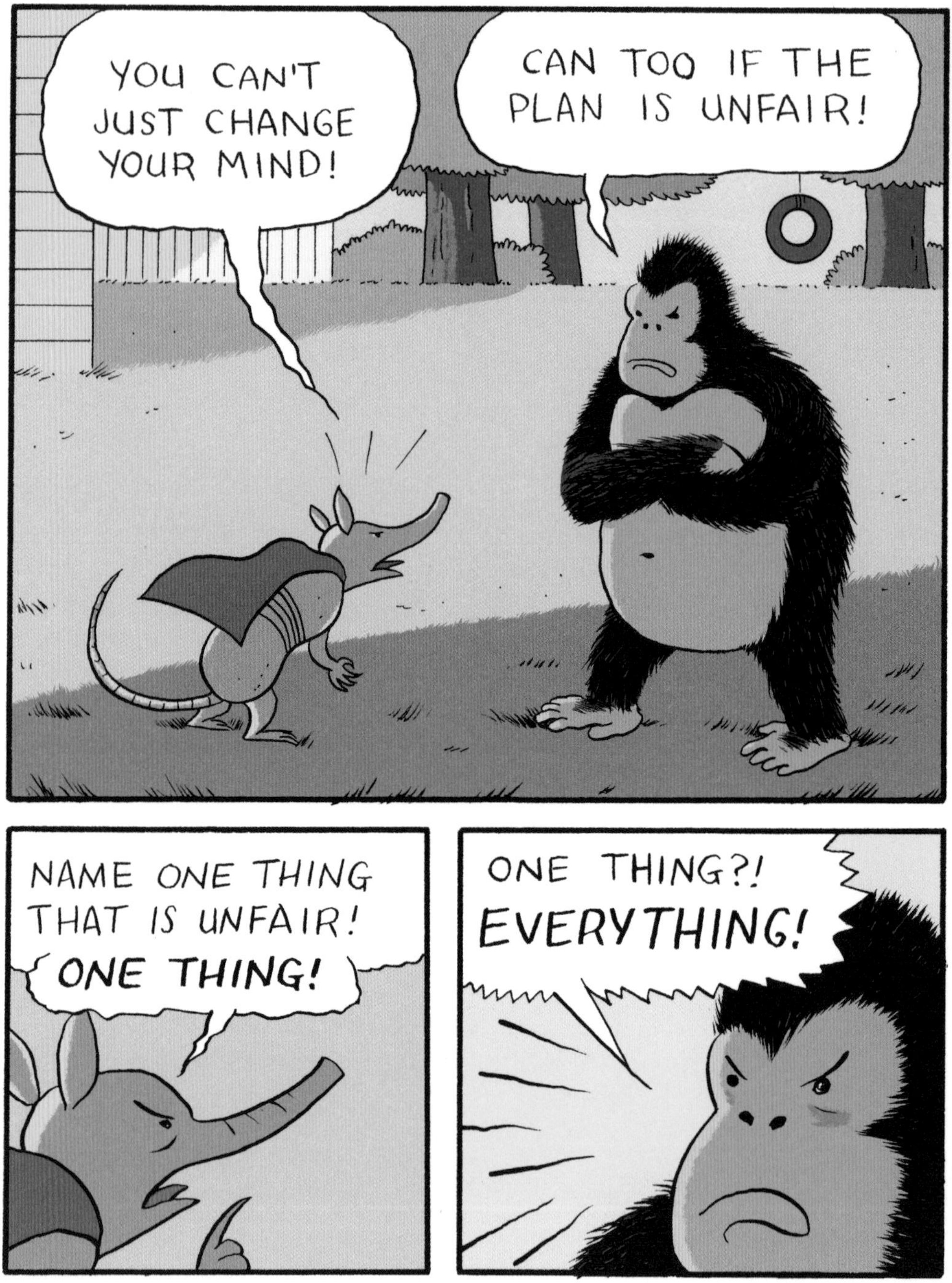
YOU CAN'T JUST CHANGE YOUR MIND!
CAN TOO IF THE PLAN IS UNFAIR!
NAME ONE THING THAT IS UNFAIR! ONE THING!
ONE THING?! EVERYTHING!

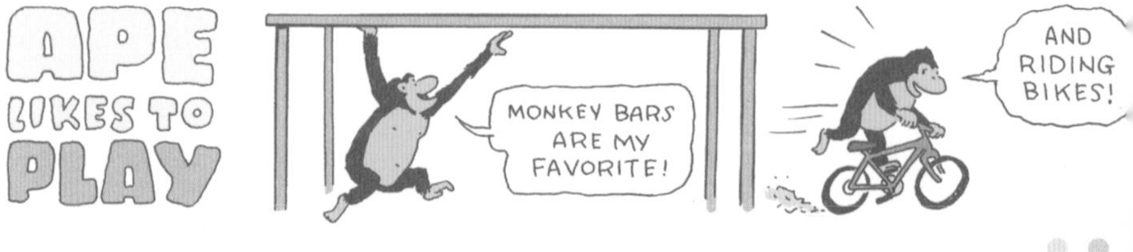
APE LIKES TO PLAY
MONKEY BARS ARE MY FAVORITE!
AND RIDING BIKES!

WHY DO I HAVE TO DISTRACT THE SPITTING SERPENT THAT GUARDS THE CASTLE...

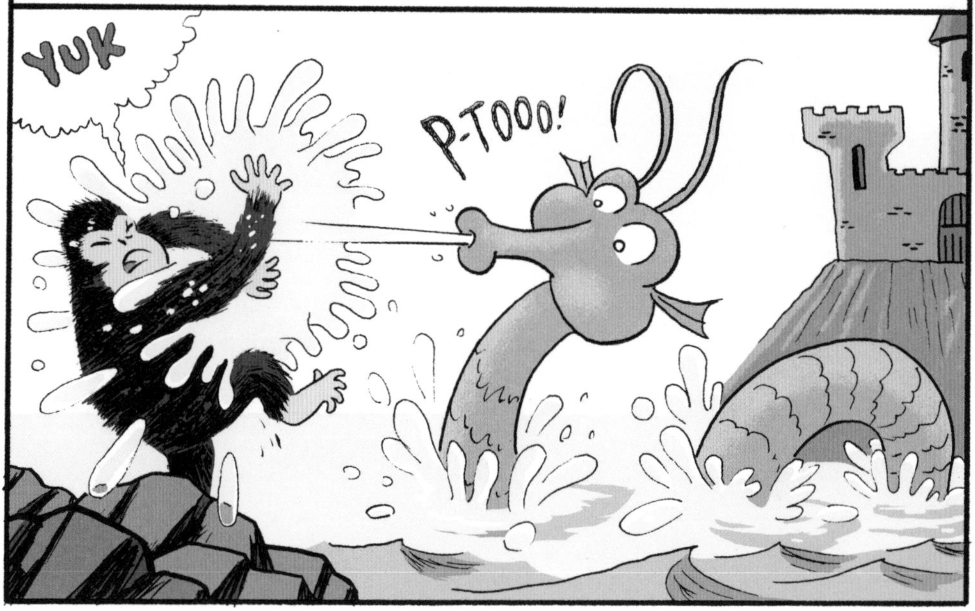
YUK
P-TOOO!

WHILE YOU SNEAK IN WITH THE PRINCESS TO STEAL THE WIZARD KING'S WAND?

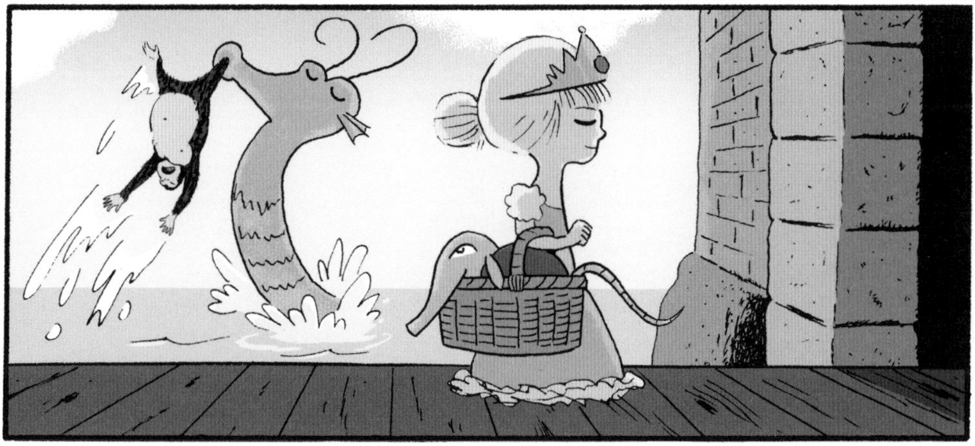

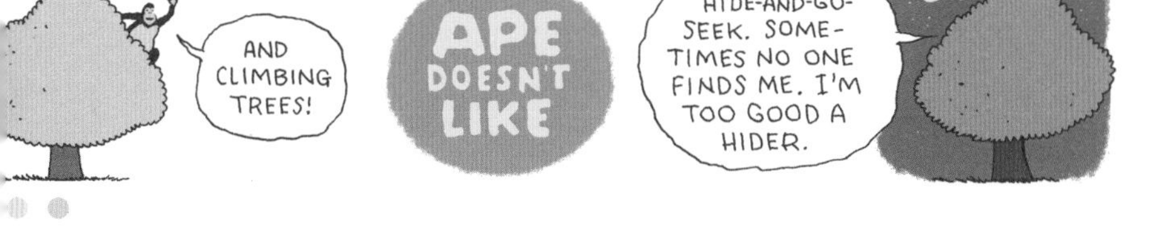
AND CLIMBING TREES!
APE DOESN'T LIKE
HIDE-AND-GO-SEEK. SOMETIMES NO ONE FINDS ME. I'M TOO GOOD A HIDER.

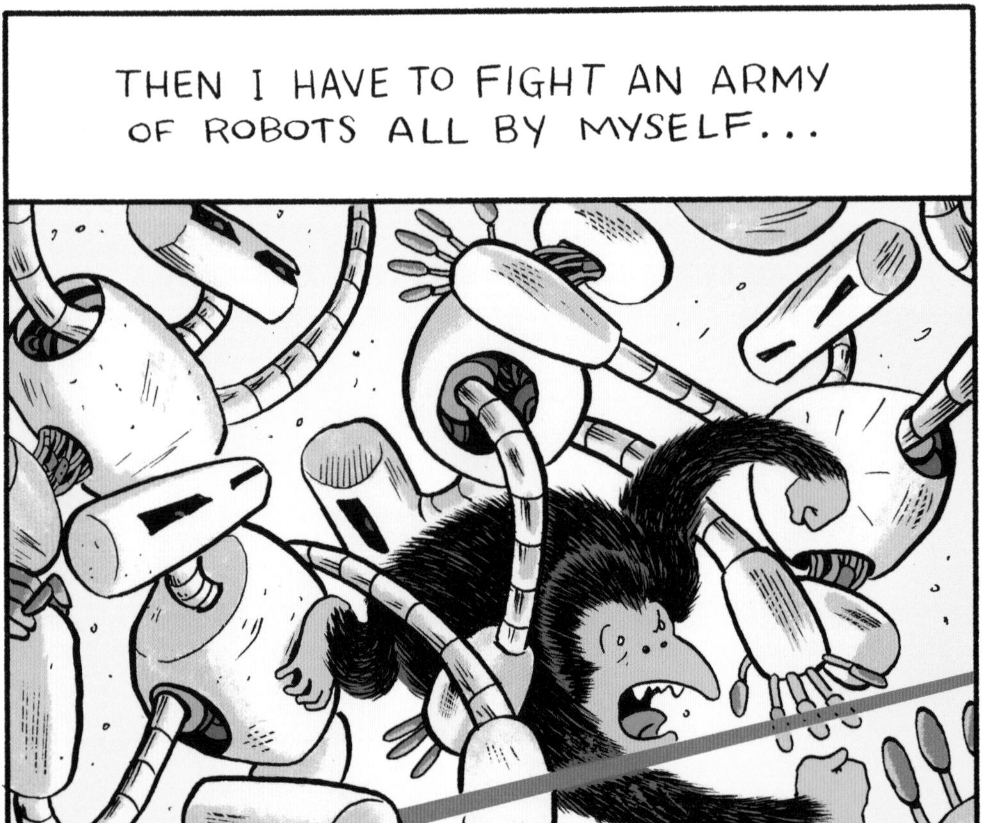
THEN I HAVE TO FIGHT AN ARMY OF ROBOTS ALL BY MYSELF...

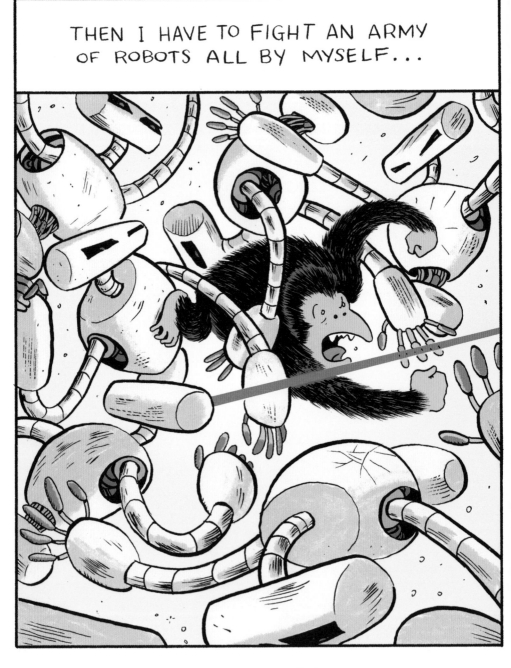

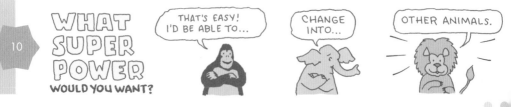

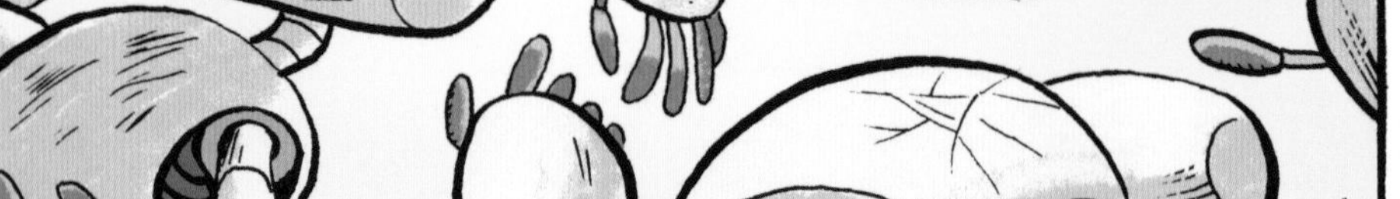
WHAT SUPER POWER WOULD YOU WANT?
THAT'S EASY! I'D BE ABLE TO...
CHANGE INTO...
OTHER ANIMALS.

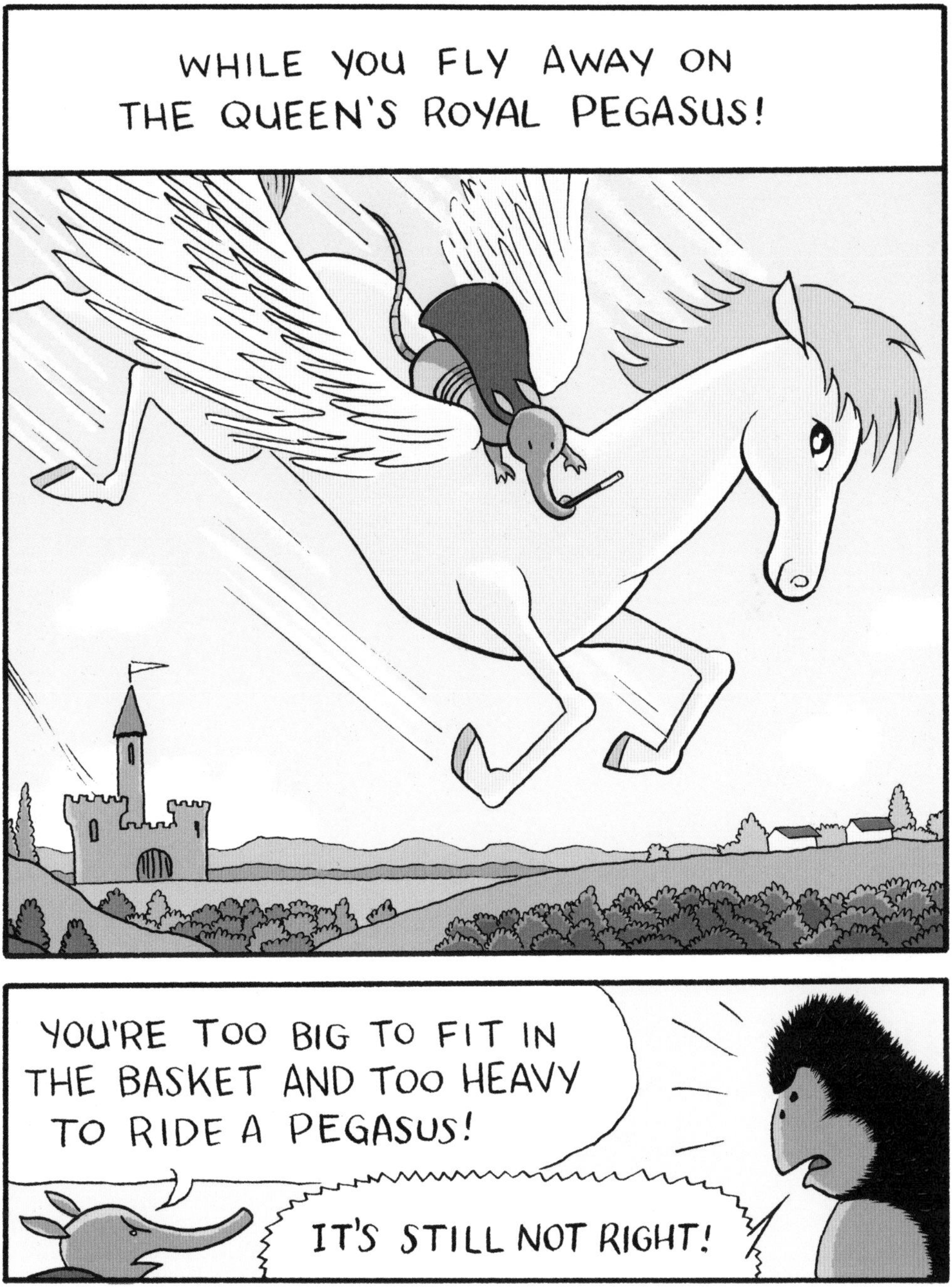
WHILE YOU FLY AWAY ON THE QUEEN'S ROYAL PEGASUS!
YOU'RE TOO BIG TO FIT IN THE BASKET AND TOO HEAVY TO RIDE A PEGASUS!
IT'S STILL NOT RIGHT!

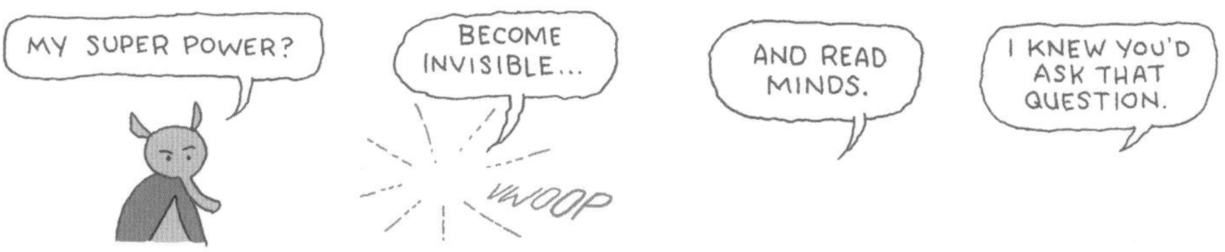
MY SUPER POWER?
BECOME INVISIBLE...
VWOOP
AND READ MINDS.
I KNEW YOU'D ASK THAT QUESTION.

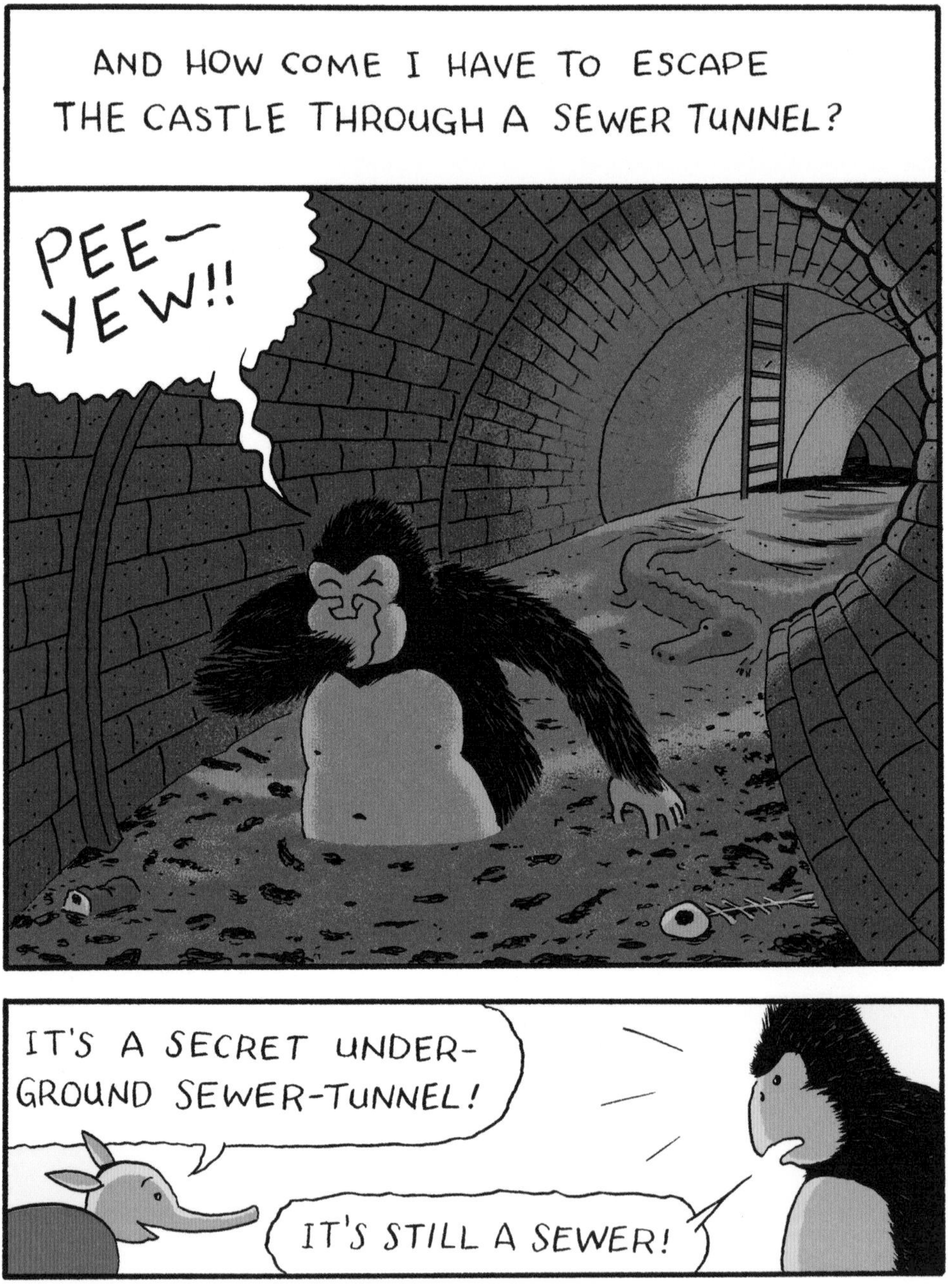

AND HOW COME I HAVE TO ESCAPE THE CASTLE THROUGH A SEWER TUNNEL?
PEE-YEW!!
IT'S A SECRET UNDER-GROUND SEWER-TUNNEL!
IT'S STILL A SEWER!

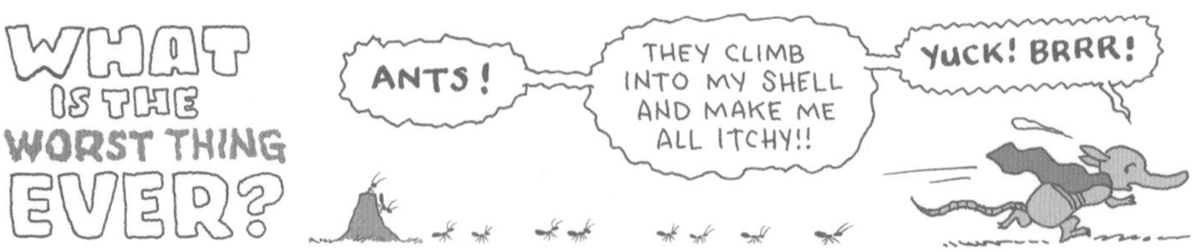

WHAT IS THE WORST THING EVER?
ANTS!
THEY CLIMB INTO MY SHELL AND MAKE ME ALL ITCHY!!
YUCK! BRRR!

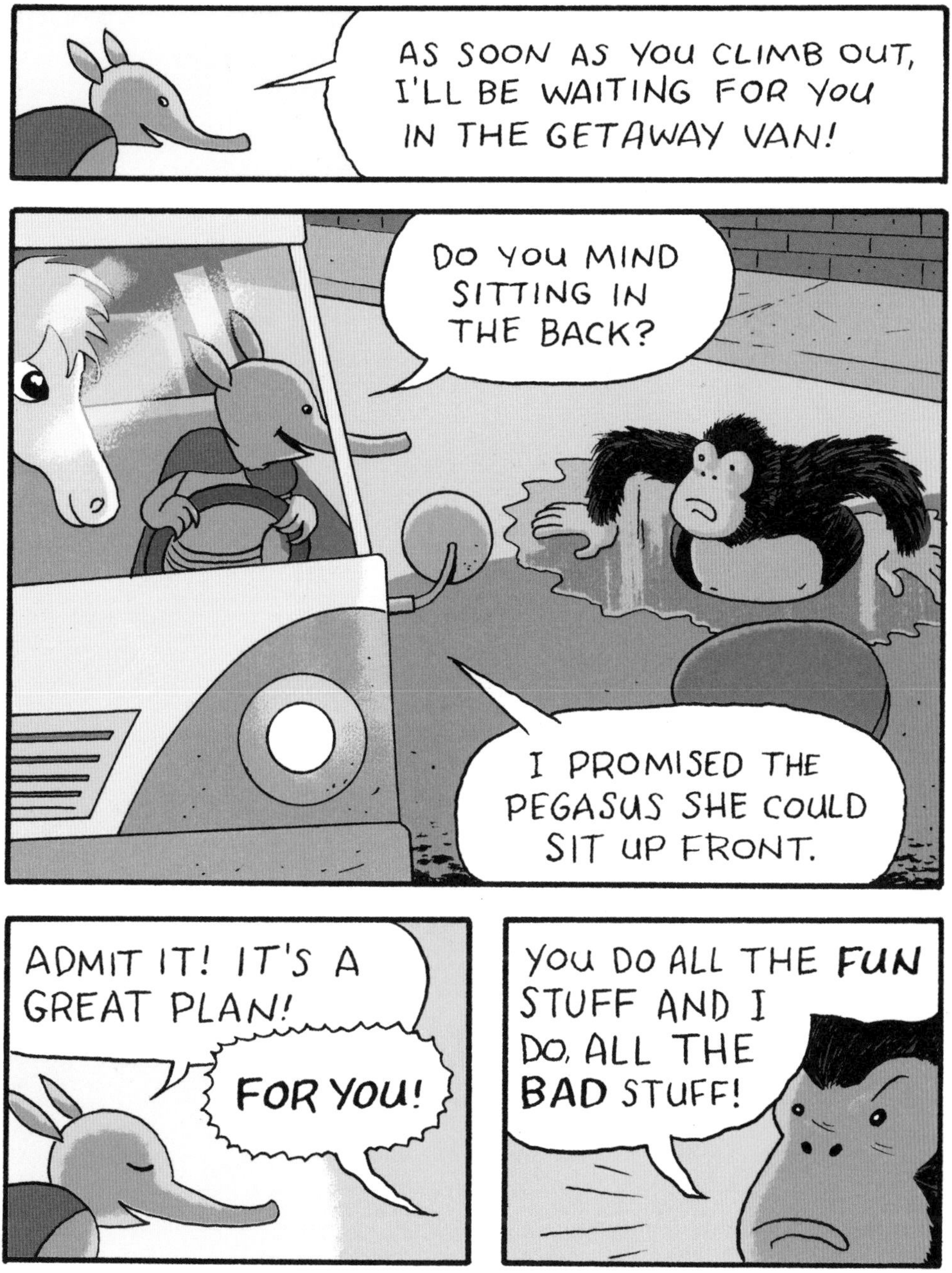
AS SOON AS YOU CLIMB OUT, I'LL BE WAITING FOR YOU IN THE GETAWAY VAN!
DO YOU MIND SITTING IN THE BACK?
I PROMISED THE PEGASUS SHE COULD SIT UP FRONT.
ADMIT IT! IT'S A GREAT PLAN!
FOR YOU!
YOU DO ALL THE FUN STUFF AND I DO, ALL THE BAD STUFF!

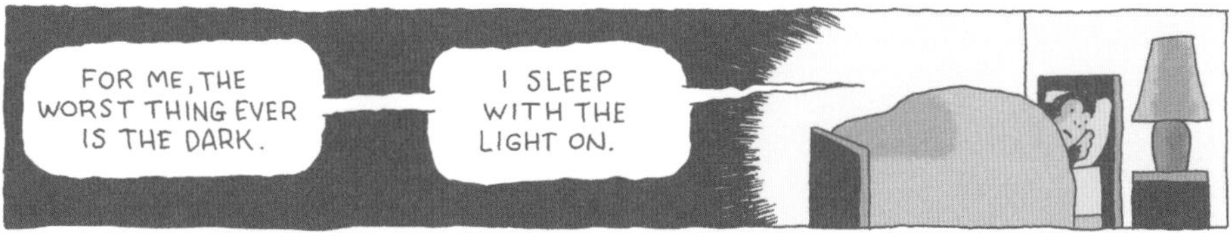
FOR ME, THE WORST THING EVER IS THE DARK.
I SLEEP WITH THE LIGHT ON.

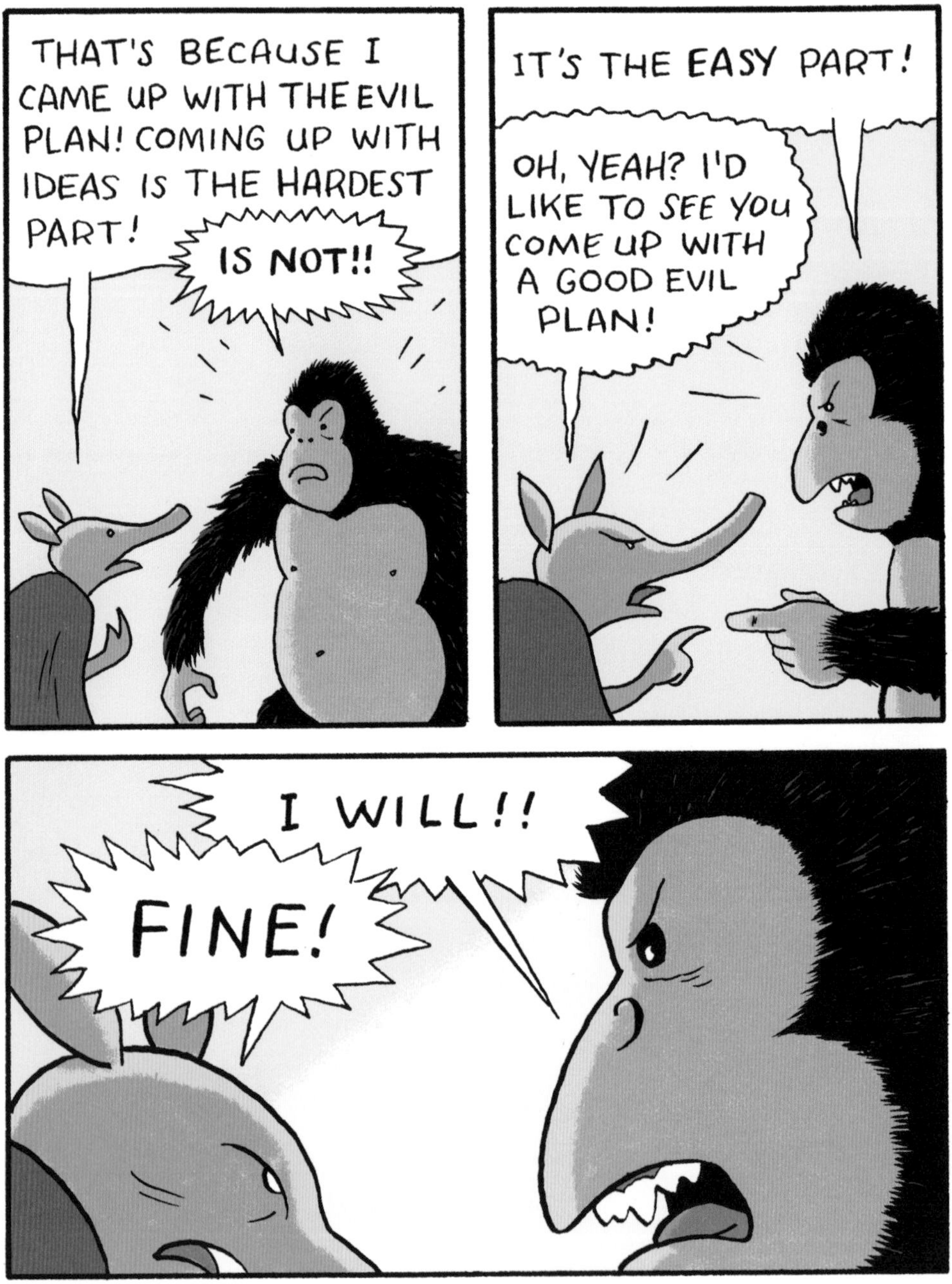
THAT'S BECAUSE I CAME UP WITH THE EVIL PLAN! COMING UP WITH IDEAS IS THE HARDEST PART!
IS NOT!!
IT'S THE EASY PART!
OH, YEAH? I'D LIKE TO SEE YOU COME UP WITH A GOOD EVIL PLAN!
I WILL!!
FINE!

IF YOUR FRIEND WAS A COOKIE WHAT KIND WOULD THEY BE?

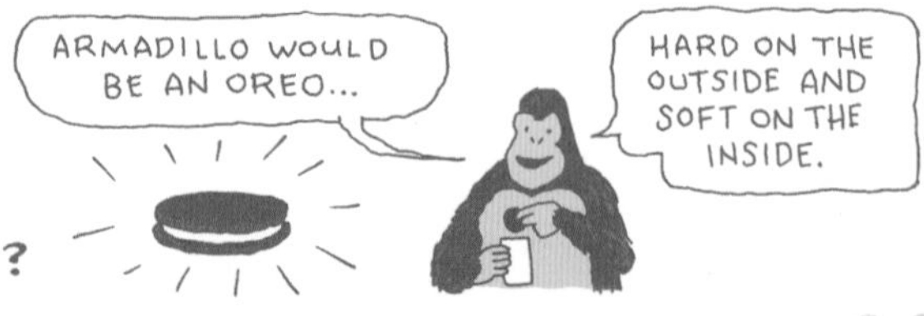
ARMADILLO WOULD BE AN OREO...
HARD ON THE OUTSIDE AND SOFT ON THE INSIDE.

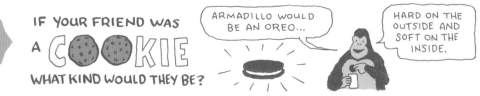

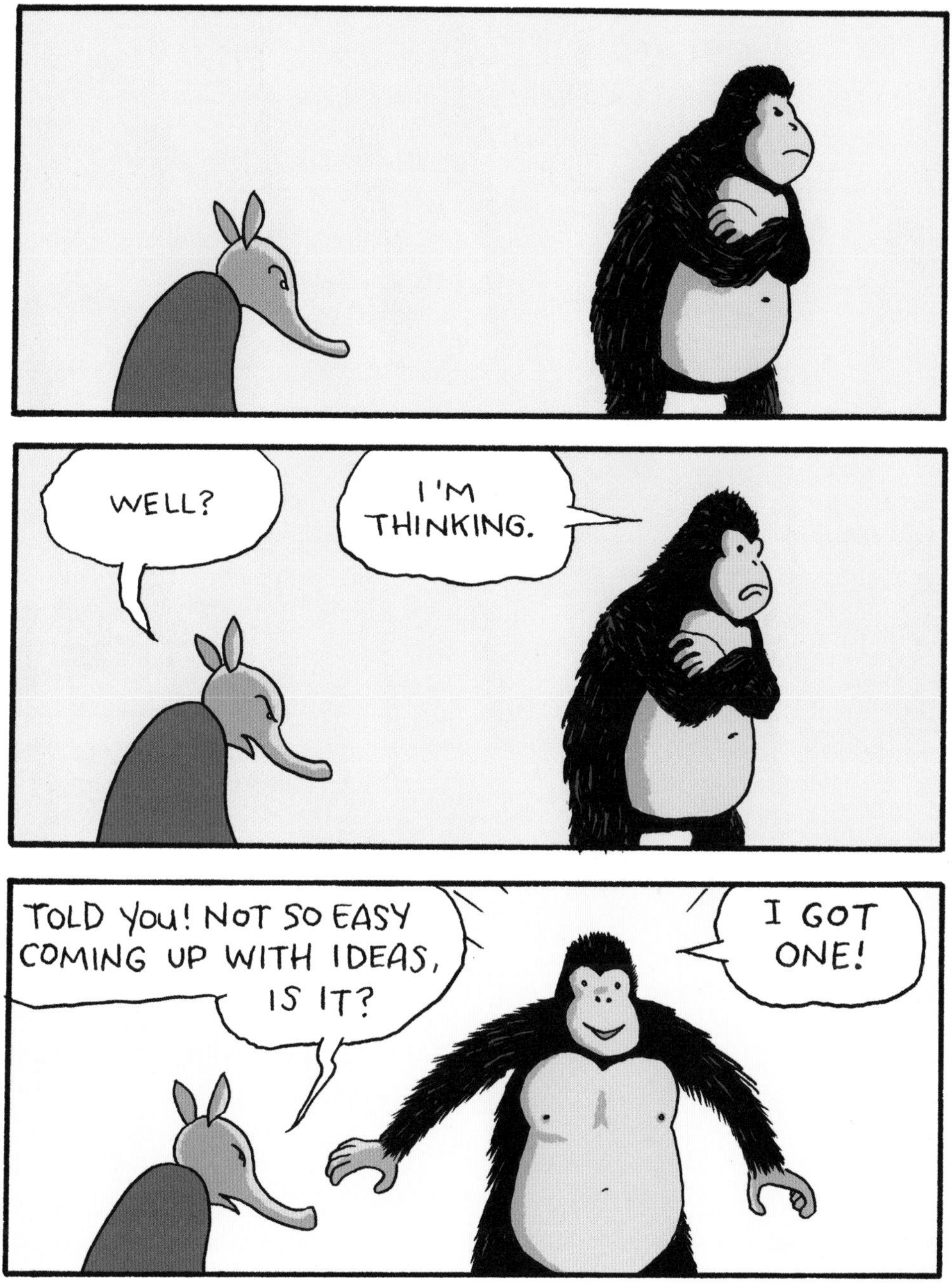
WELL?
I'M THINKING.
TOLD YOU! NOT SO EASY COMING UP WITH IDEAS, IS IT?
I GOT ONE!

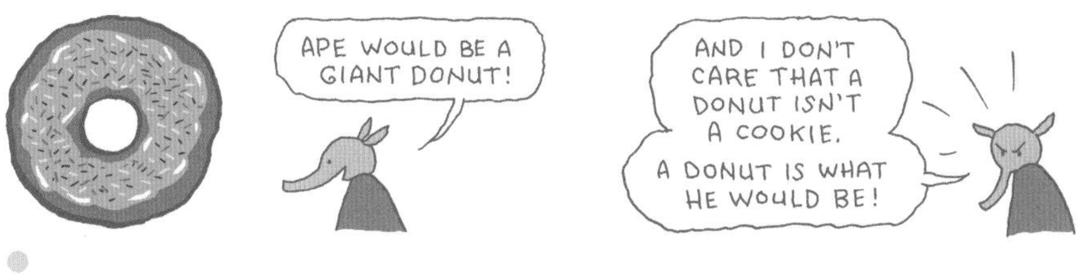
APE WOULD BE A GIANT DONUT!
AND I DON'T CARE THAT A DONUT ISN'T A COOKIE.
A DONUT IS WHAT HE WOULD BE!

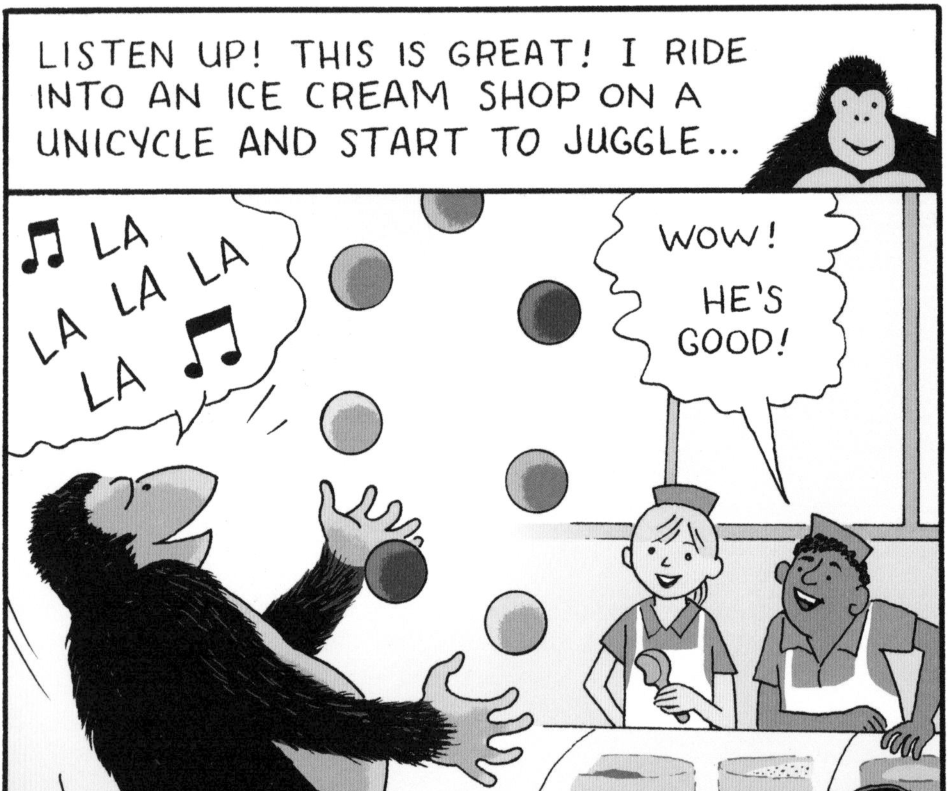
LISTEN UP! THIS IS GREAT! I RIDE INTO AN ICE CREAM SHOP ON A UNICYCLE AND START TO JUGGLE...
♫ LA LA LA LA LA ♫
WOW! HE'S GOOD!
GO, APE, GO!

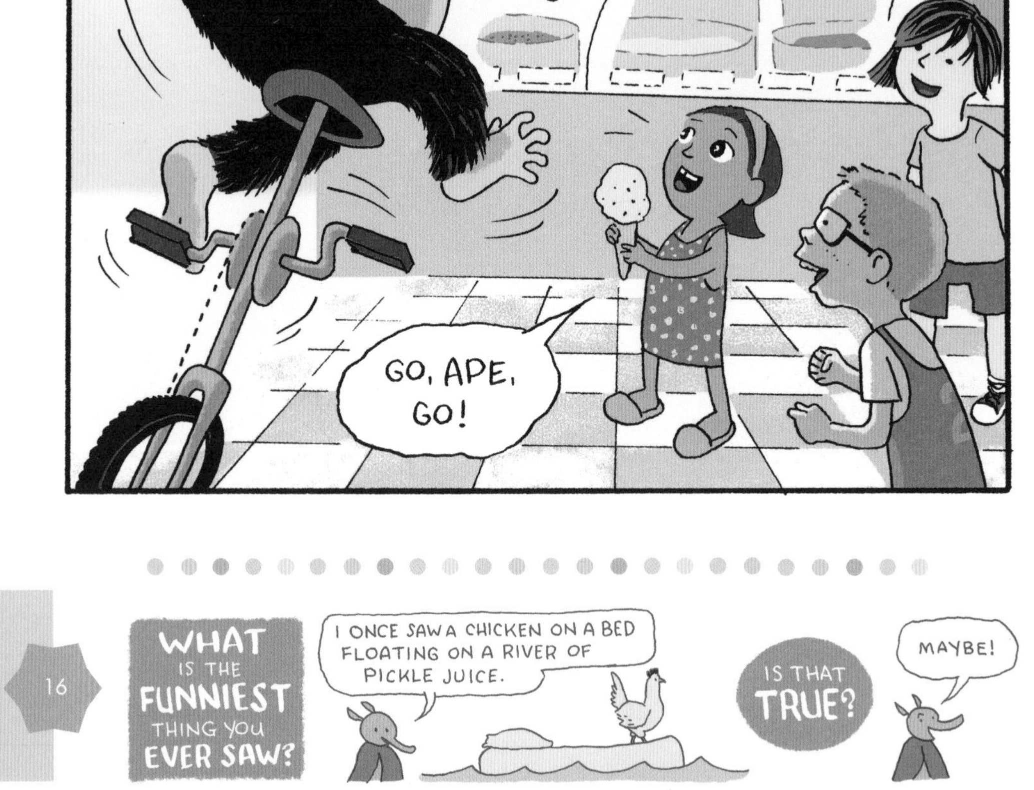
WHAT IS THE FUNNIEST THING YOU EVER SAW?
I ONCE SAW A CHICKEN ON A BED FLOATING ON A RIVER OF PICKLE JUICE.
IS THAT TRUE?
MAYBE!

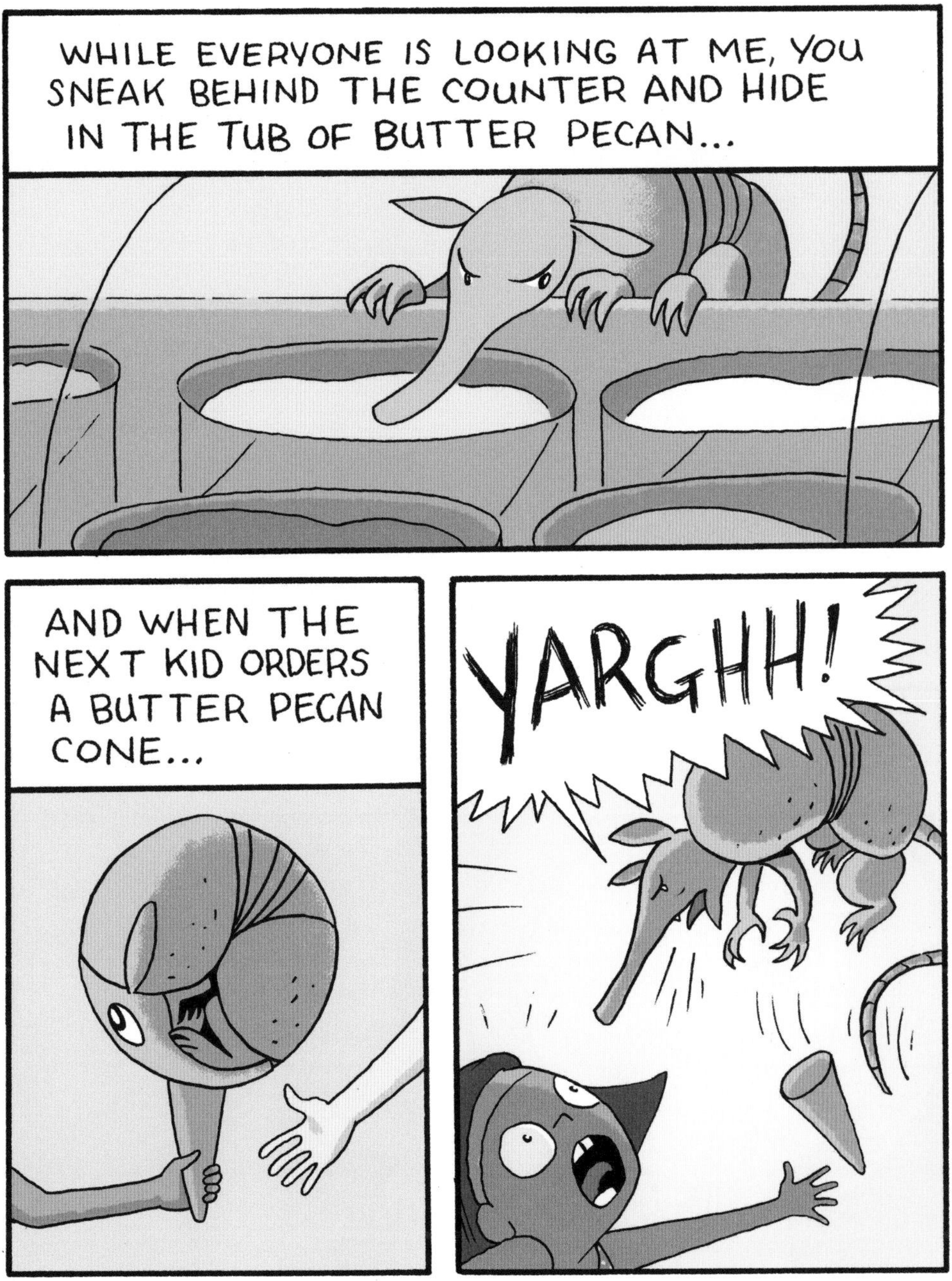
WHILE EVERYONE IS LOOKING AT ME, YOU SNEAK BEHIND THE COUNTER AND HIDE IN THE TUB OF BUTTER PECAN...
AND WHEN THE NEXT KID ORDERS A BUTTER PECAN CONE...
YARGHH!

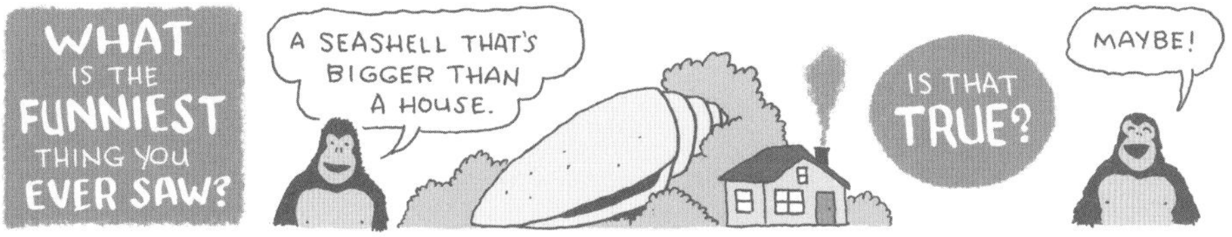
WHAT IS THE FUNNIEST THING YOU EVER SAW?
A SEASHELL THAT'S BIGGER THAN A HOUSE.
IS THAT TRUE?
MAYBE!

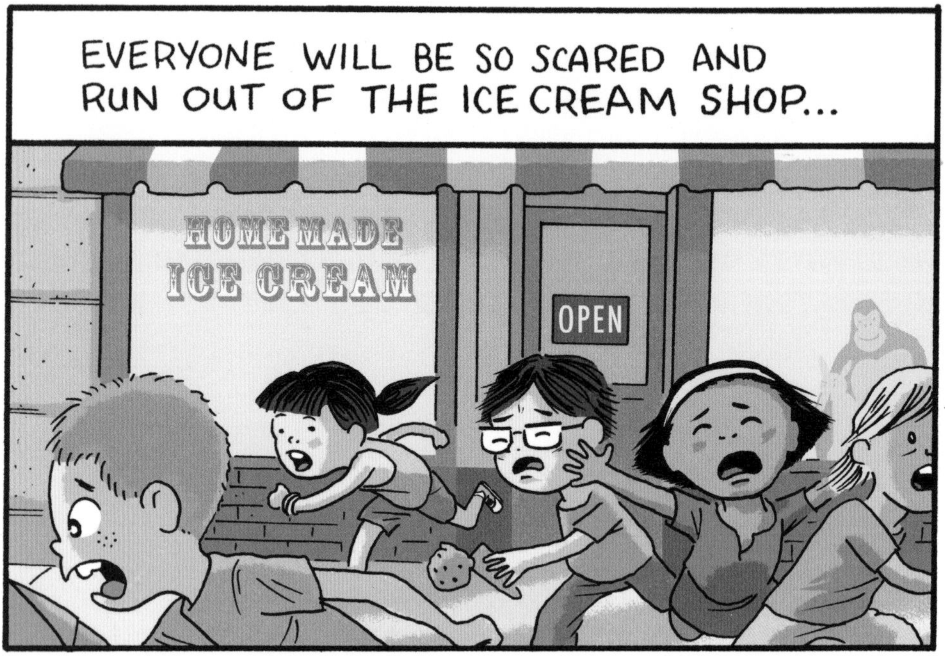
EVERYONE WILL BE SO SCARED AND RUN OUT OF THE ICE CREAM SHOP...
HOMEMADE ICE CREAM
OPEN

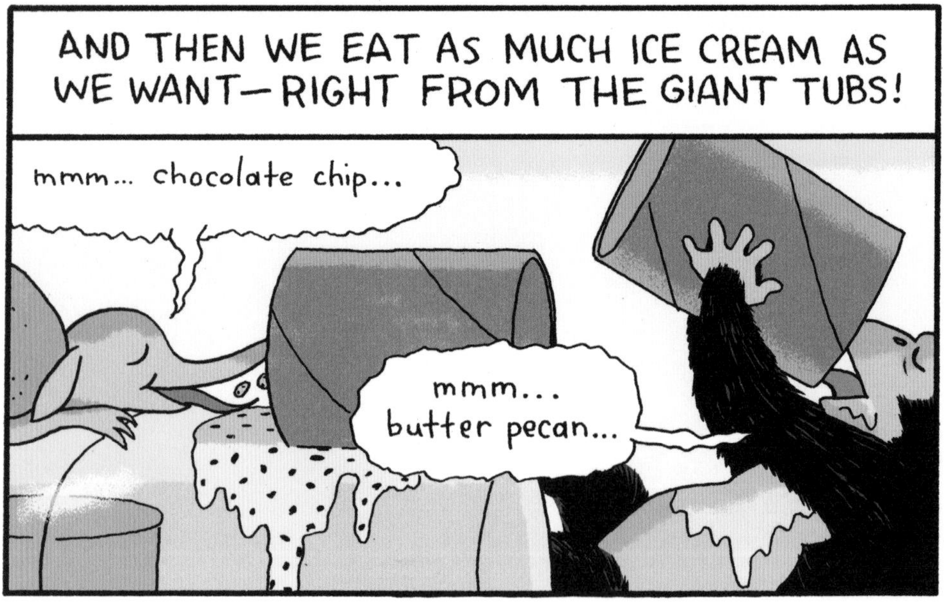
AND THEN WE EAT AS MUCH ICE CREAM AS WE WANT—RIGHT FROM THE GIANT TUBS!
mmm... chocolate chip...
mmm... butter pecan...

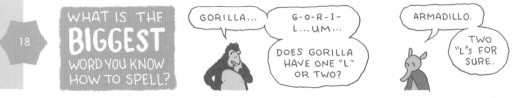

WHAT IS THE **BIGGEST** WORD YOU KNOW HOW TO SPELL?

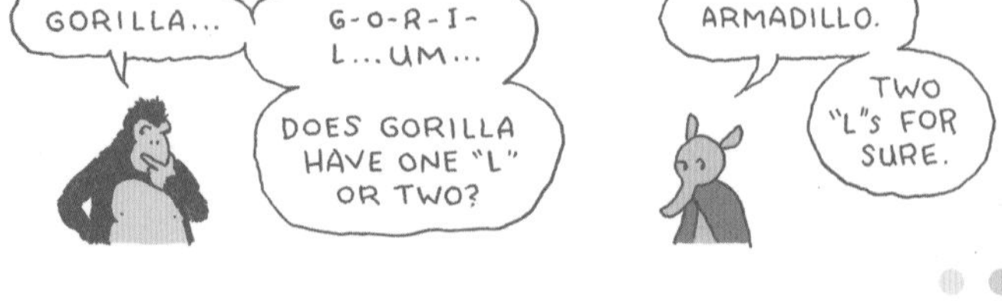
GORILLA...
G-O-R-I-L...UM...
DOES GORILLA HAVE ONE "L" OR TWO?
ARMADILLO.
TWO "L"s FOR SURE.

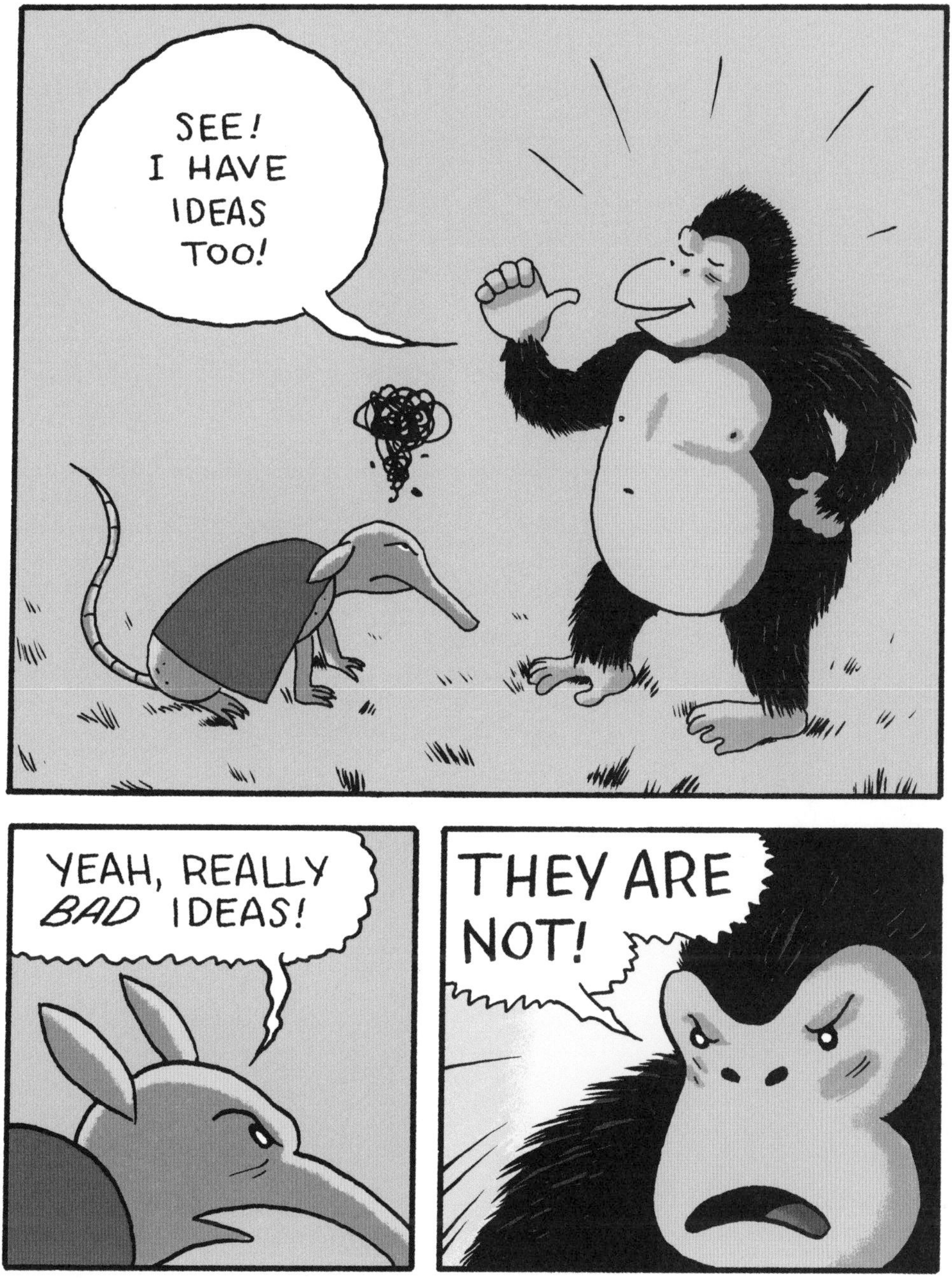
SEE! I HAVE IDEAS TOO!
YEAH, REALLY *BAD* IDEAS!
THEY ARE NOT!

WHAT IS THE SMALLEST WORD YOU CAN SPELL?

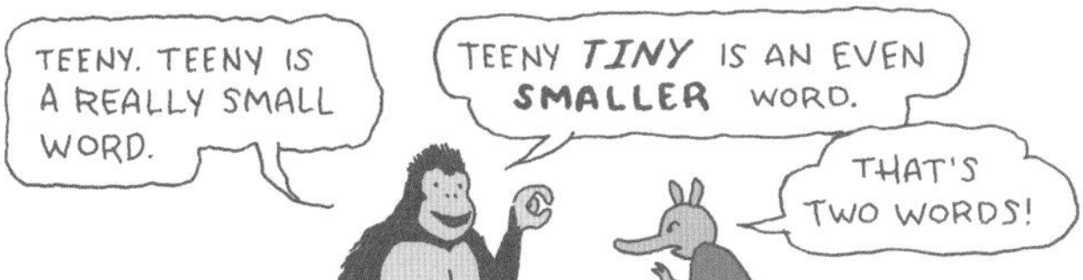
TEENY. TEENY IS A REALLY SMALL WORD.
TEENY *TINY* IS AN EVEN **SMALLER** WORD.
THAT'S TWO WORDS!

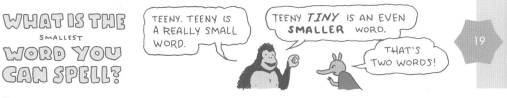

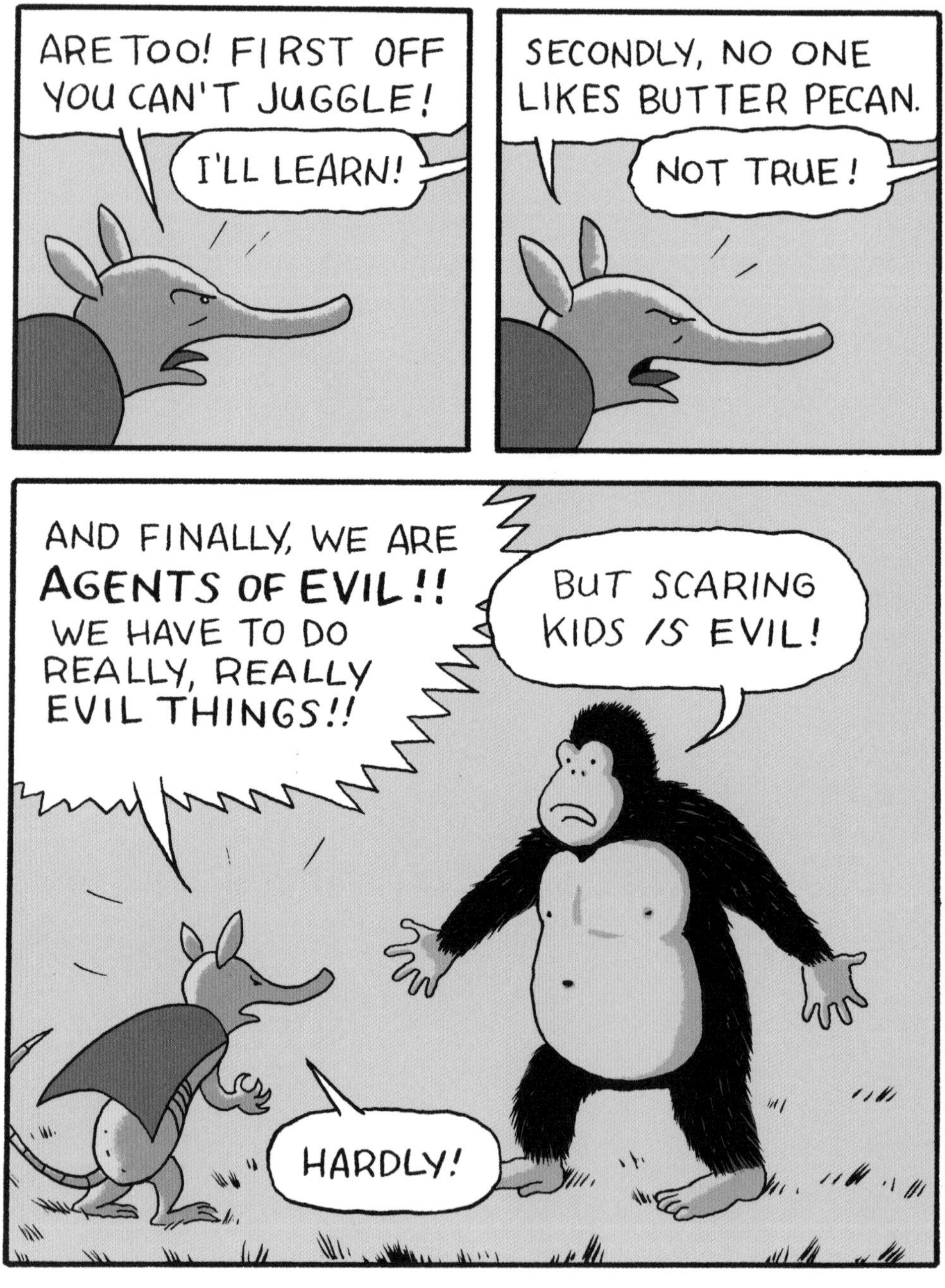
ARE TOO! FIRST OFF YOU CAN'T JUGGLE!
I'LL LEARN!
SECONDLY, NO ONE LIKES BUTTER PECAN.
NOT TRUE!
AND FINALLY, WE ARE AGENTS OF EVIL!! WE HAVE TO DO REALLY, REALLY EVIL THINGS!!
BUT SCARING KIDS IS EVIL!
HARDLY!

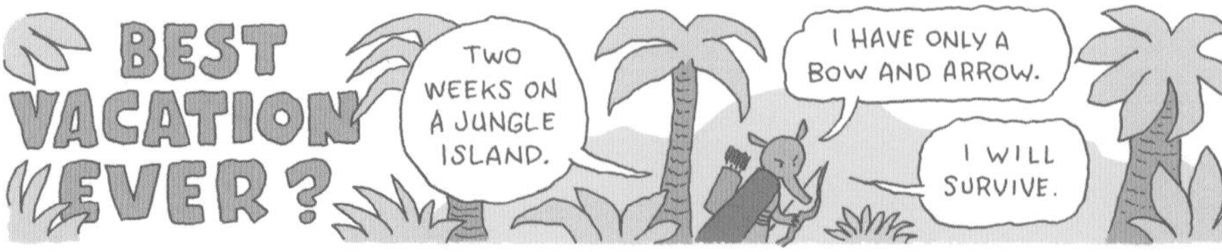
BEST VACATION EVER?
TWO WEEKS ON A JUNGLE ISLAND.
I HAVE ONLY A BOW AND ARROW.
I WILL SURVIVE.

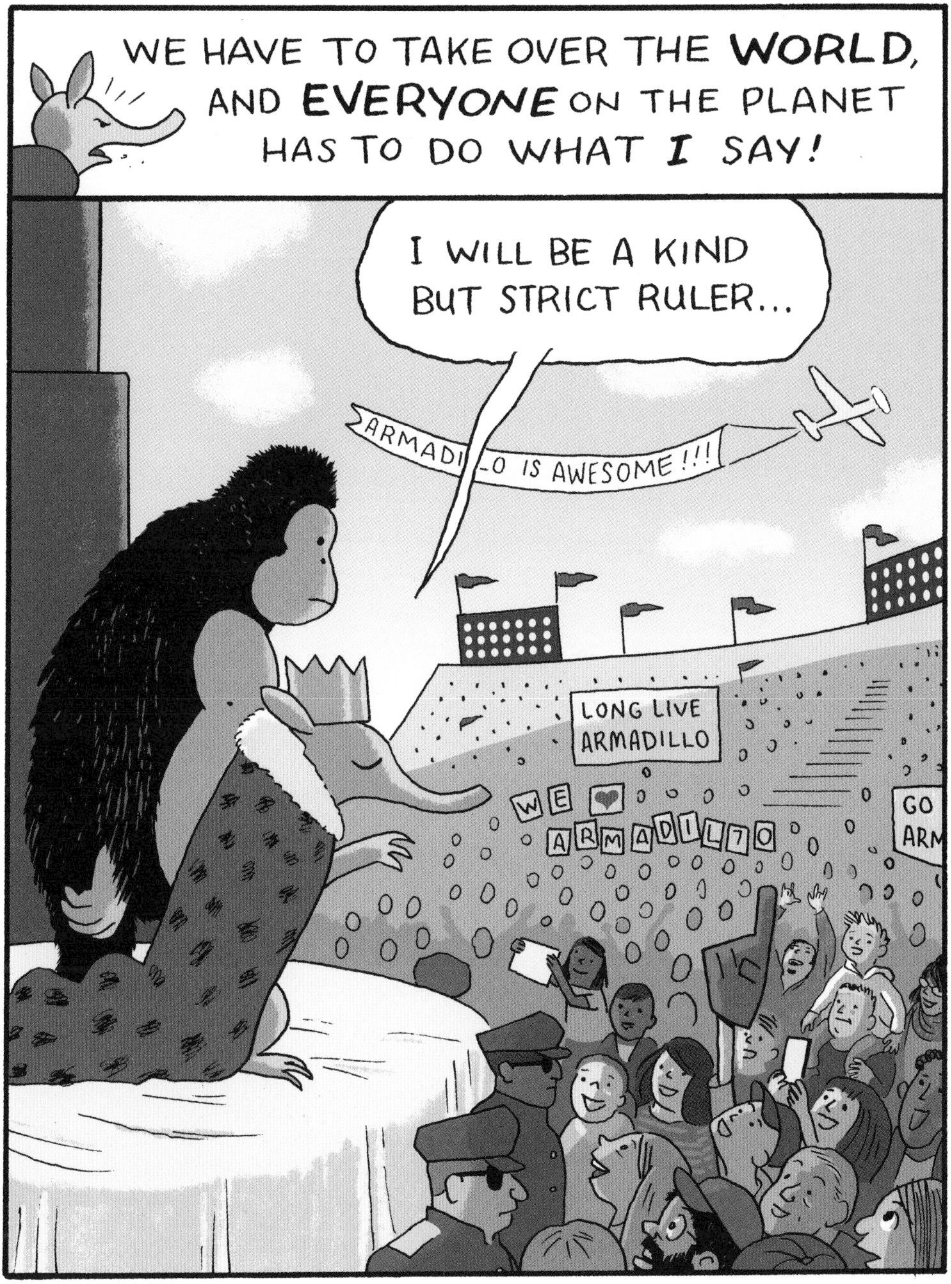
WE HAVE TO TAKE OVER THE WORLD, AND EVERYONE ON THE PLANET HAS TO DO WHAT I SAY!
I WILL BE A KIND BUT STRICT RULER...
ARMADI LO IS AWESOME!!!
LONG LIVE ARMADILLO
WE ♥ ARMADILLO
GO ARM

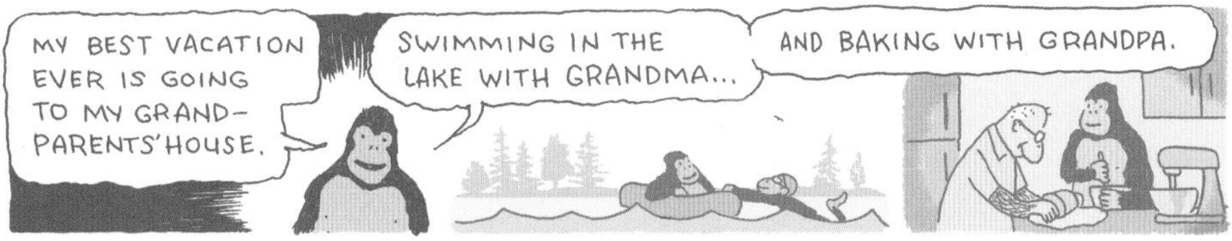
MY BEST VACATION EVER IS GOING TO MY GRAND-PARENTS' HOUSE.
SWIMMING IN THE LAKE WITH GRANDMA...
AND BAKING WITH GRANDPA.

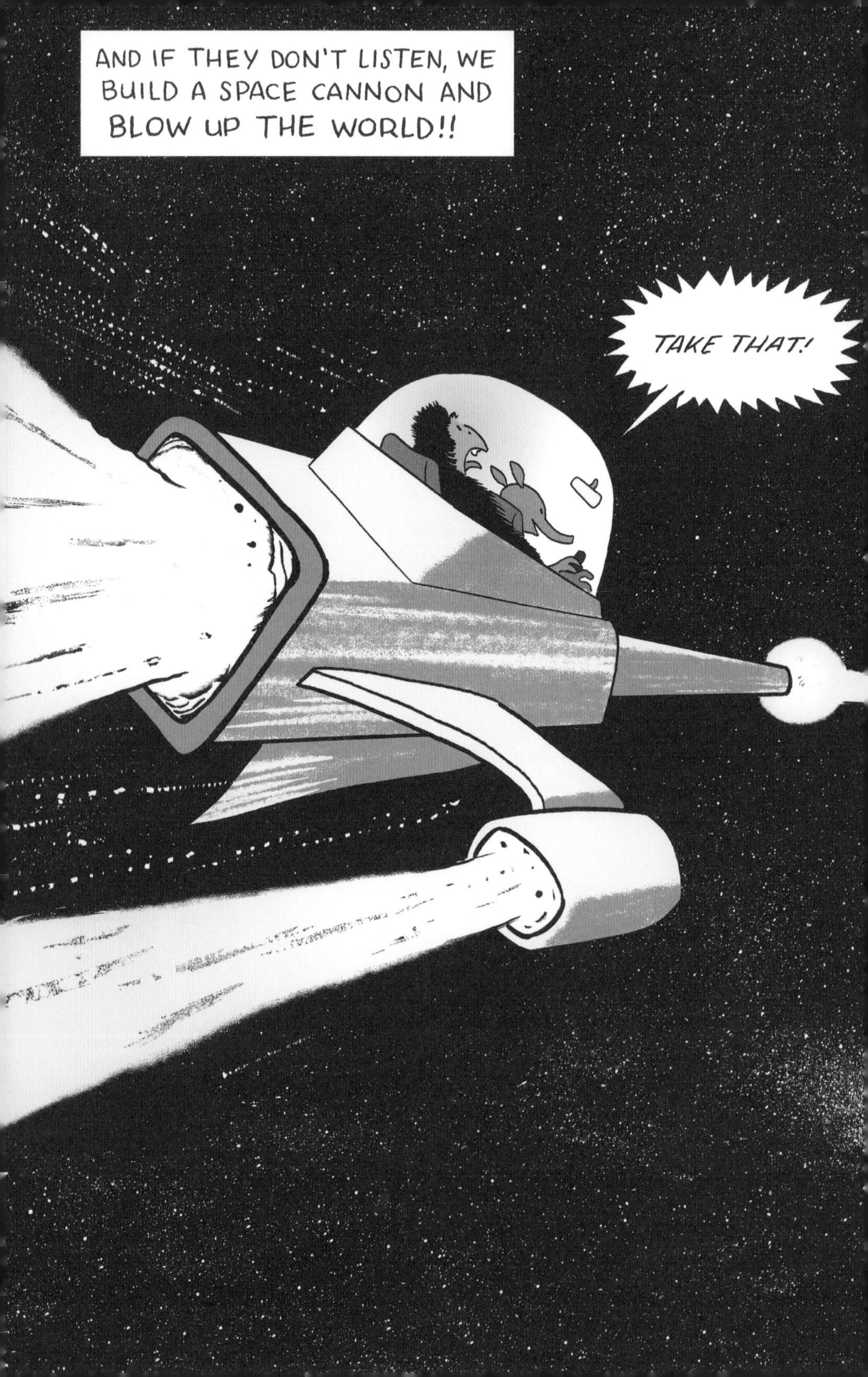
AND IF THEY DON'T LISTEN, WE BUILD A SPACE CANNON AND BLOW UP THE WORLD!!
TAKE THAT!

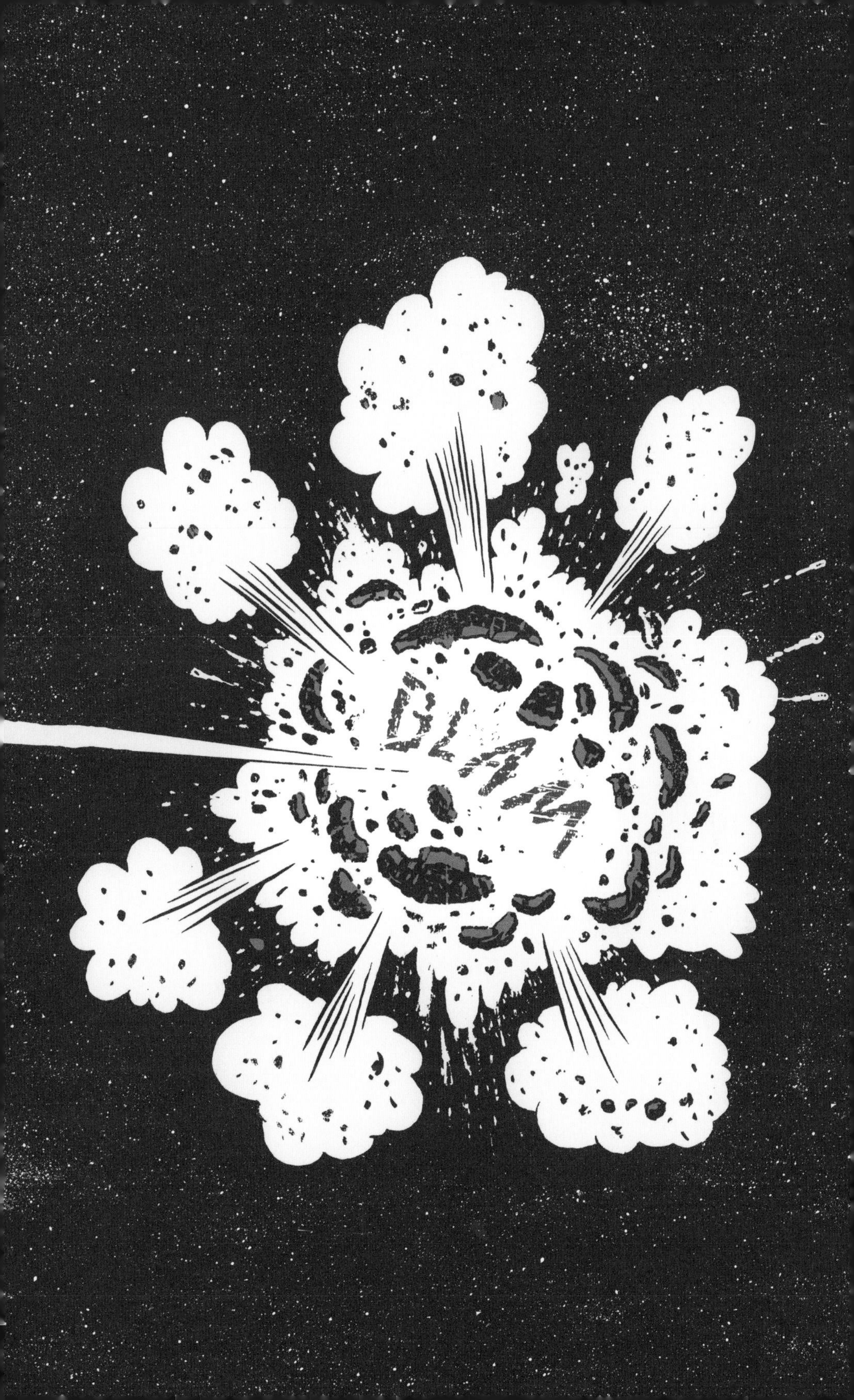
BLAM

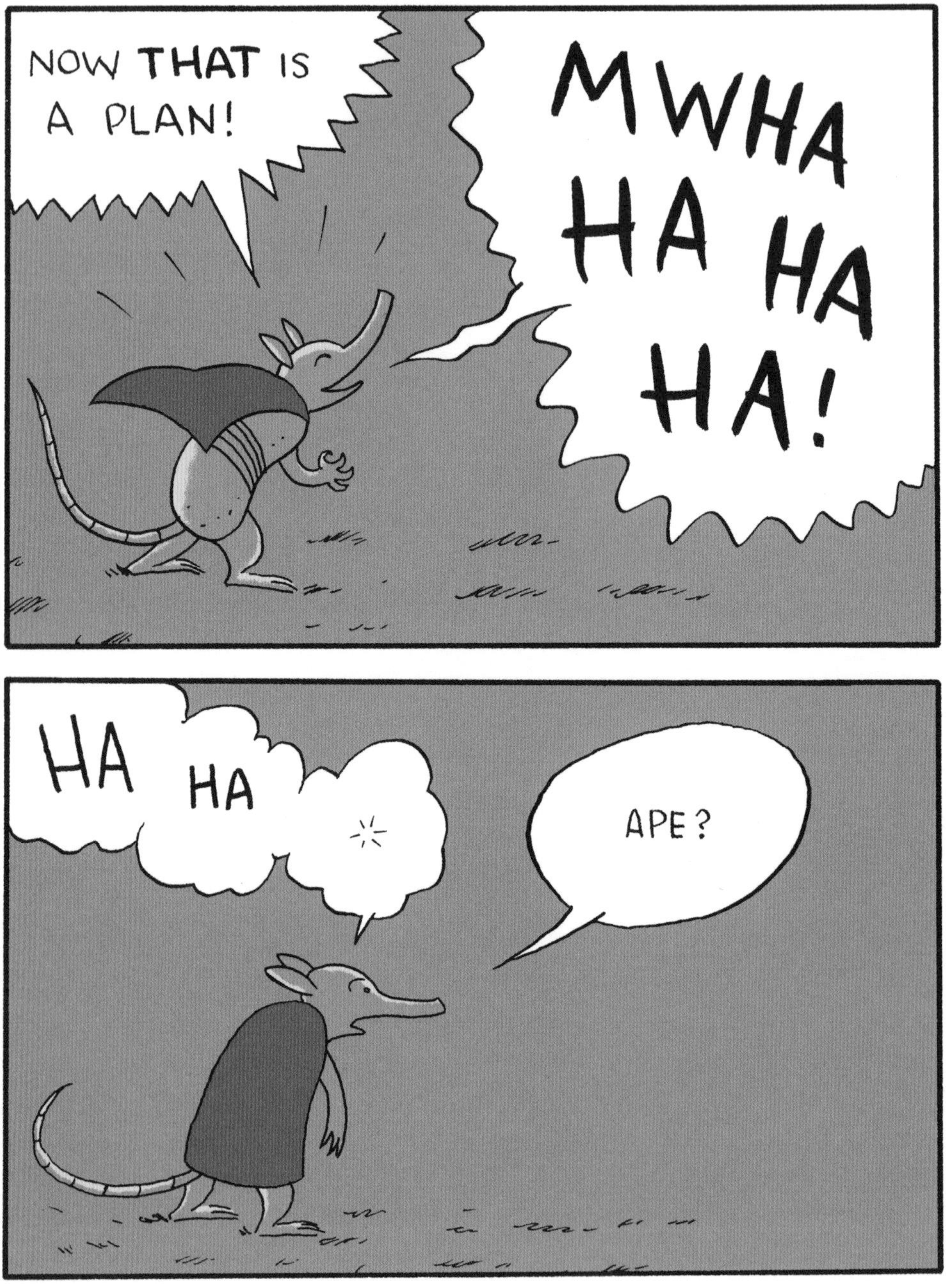
NOW **THAT** IS A PLAN!
MWHA HA HA HA!
HA HA
APE?

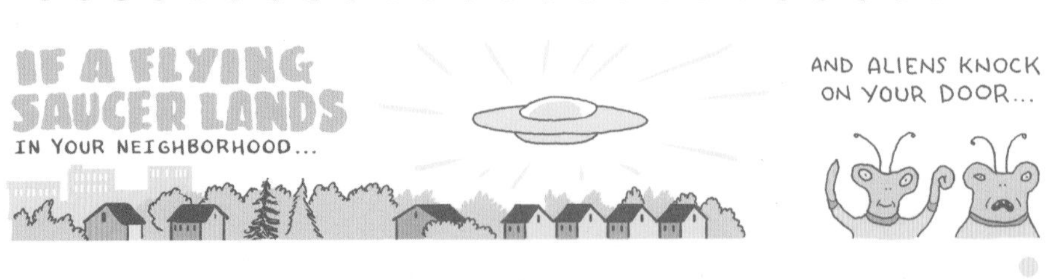
IF A FLYING SAUCER LANDS IN YOUR NEIGHBORHOOD...
AND ALIENS KNOCK ON YOUR DOOR...

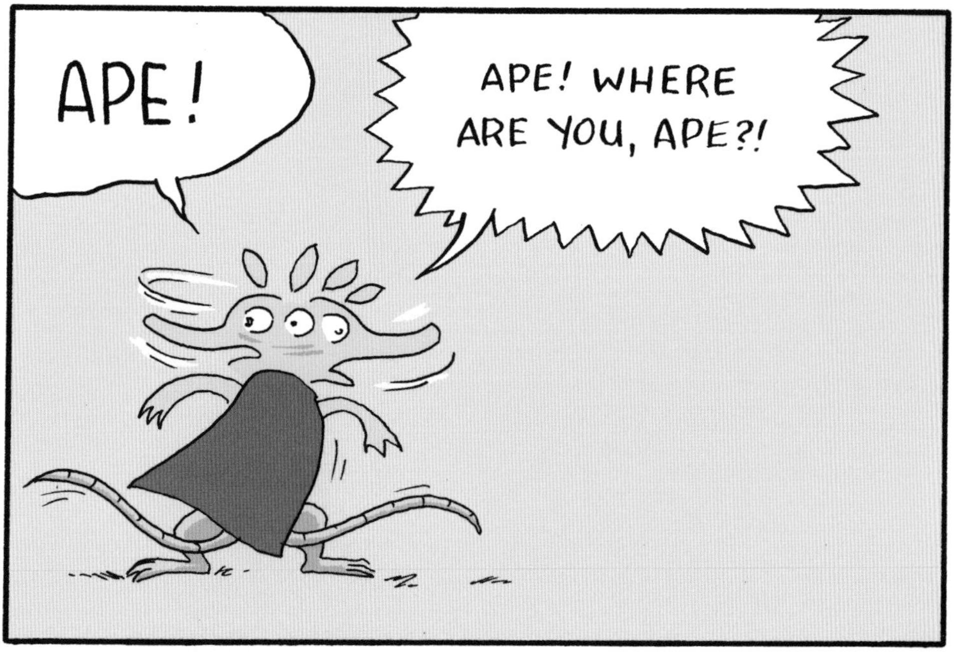
APE!
APE! WHERE ARE YOU, APE?!

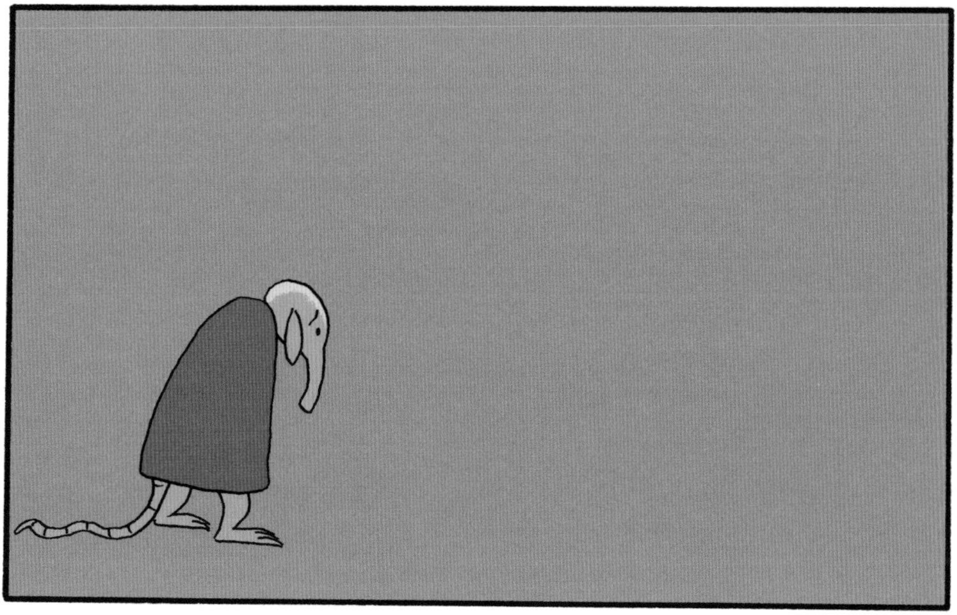

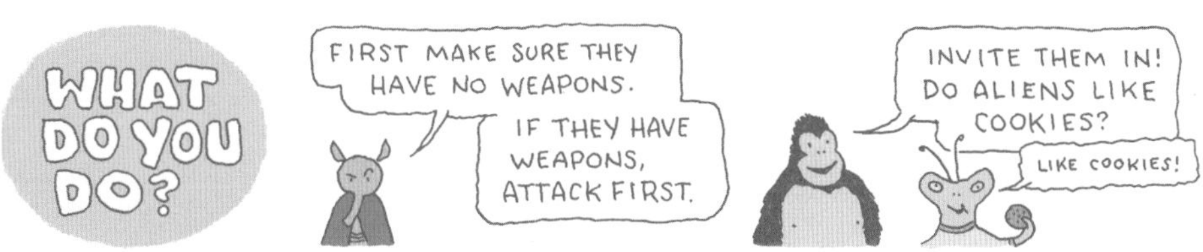
WHAT DO YOU DO?
FIRST MAKE SURE THEY HAVE NO WEAPONS.
IF THEY HAVE WEAPONS, ATTACK FIRST.
INVITE THEM IN! DO ALIENS LIKE COOKIES?
LIKE COOKIES!

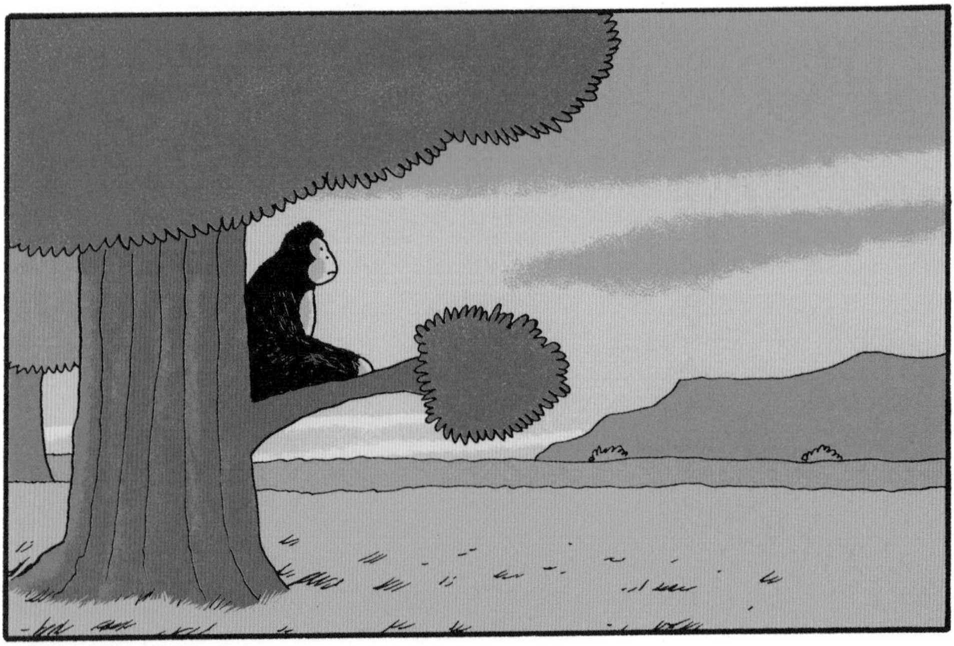

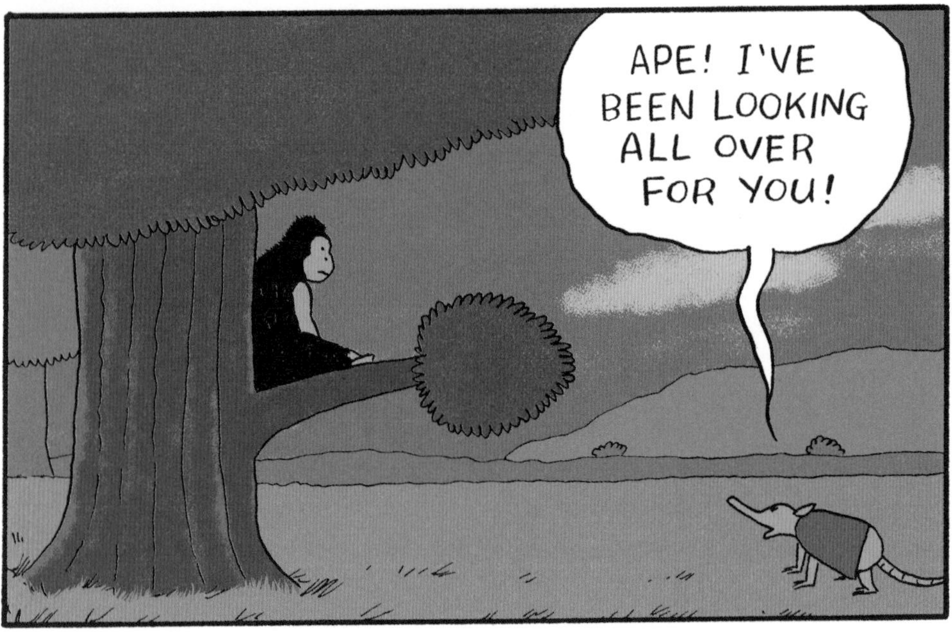
APE! I'VE BEEN LOOKING ALL OVER FOR YOU!

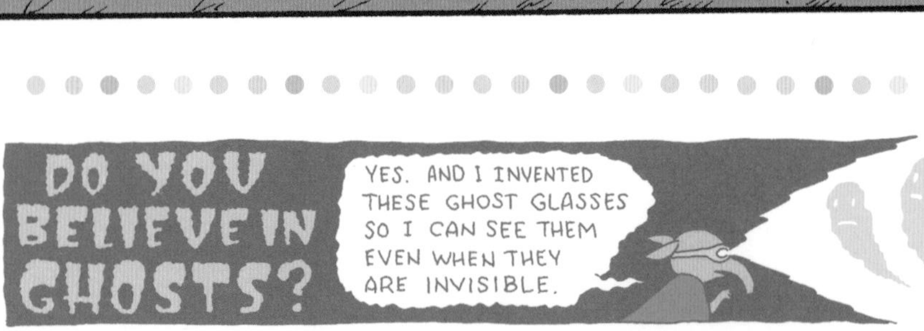
DO YOU BELIEVE IN GHOSTS?
YES. AND I INVENTED THESE GHOST GLASSES SO I CAN SEE THEM EVEN WHEN THEY ARE INVISIBLE.

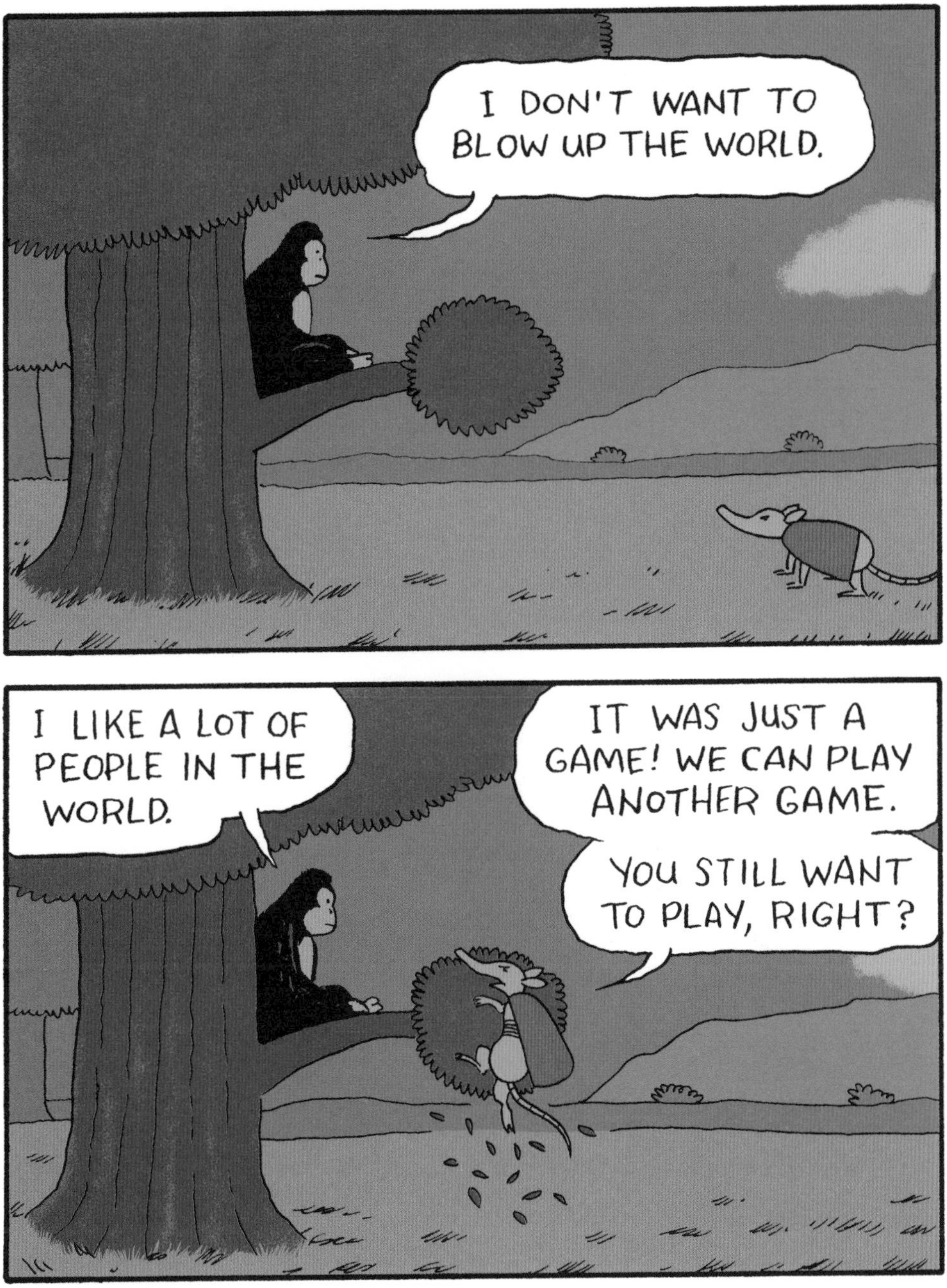
I DON'T WANT TO BLOW UP THE WORLD.
I LIKE A LOT OF PEOPLE IN THE WORLD.
IT WAS JUST A GAME! WE CAN PLAY ANOTHER GAME.
YOU STILL WANT TO PLAY, RIGHT?

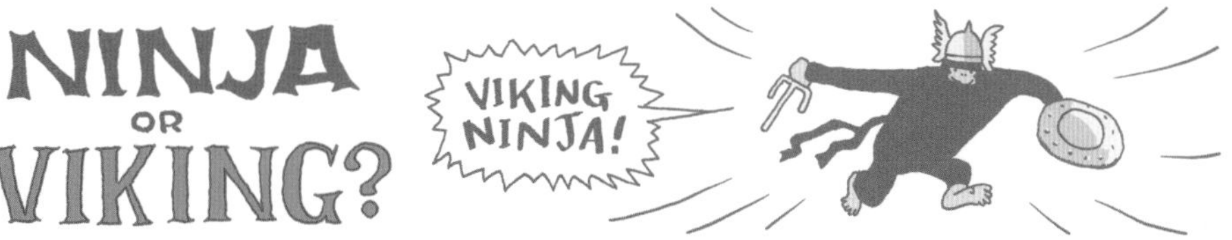
NINJA OR VIKING?
VIKING NINJA!

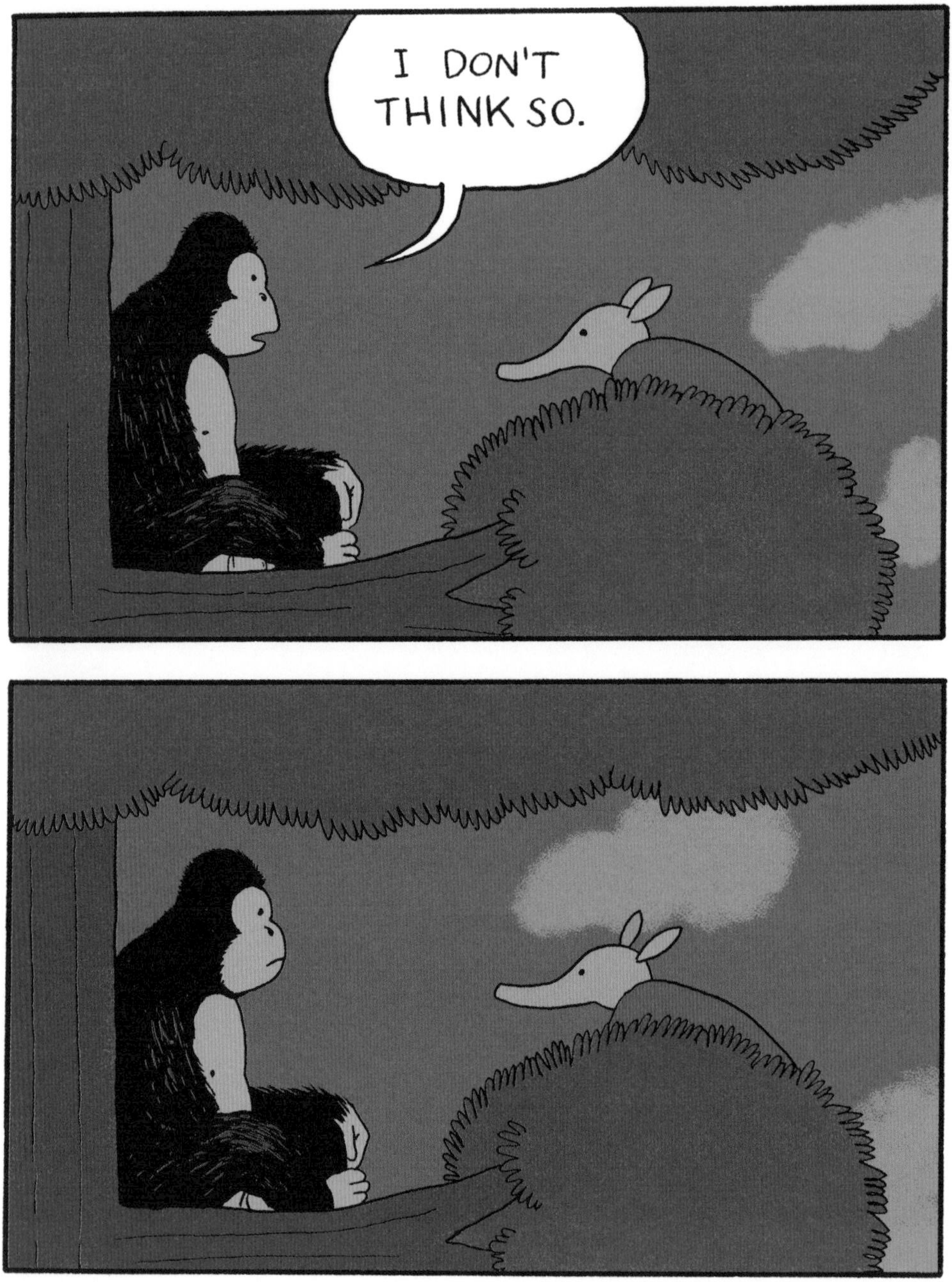
I DON'T THINK SO.

YOUR GREATEST INVENTION

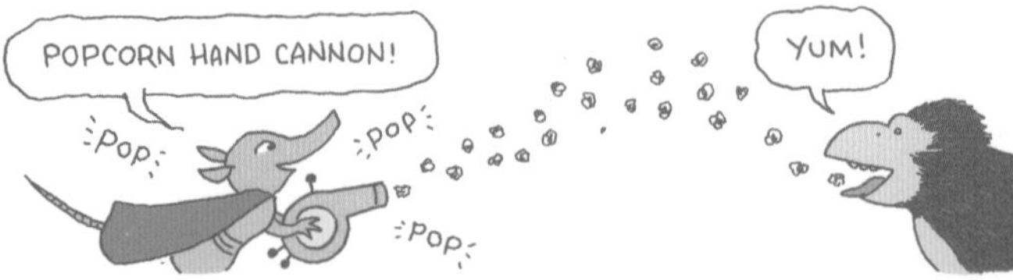
POPCORN HAND CANNON!
POP
POP
POP
YUM!

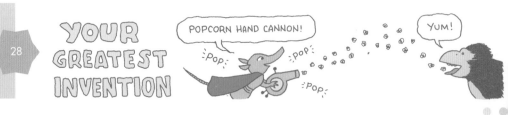

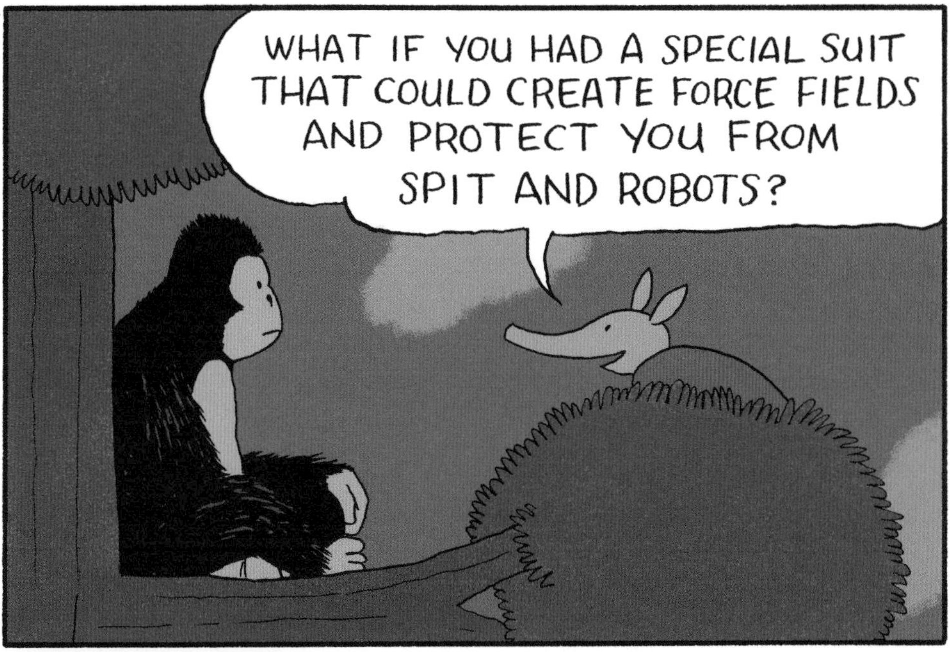
WHAT IF YOU HAD A SPECIAL SUIT THAT COULD CREATE FORCE FIELDS AND PROTECT YOU FROM SPIT AND ROBOTS?

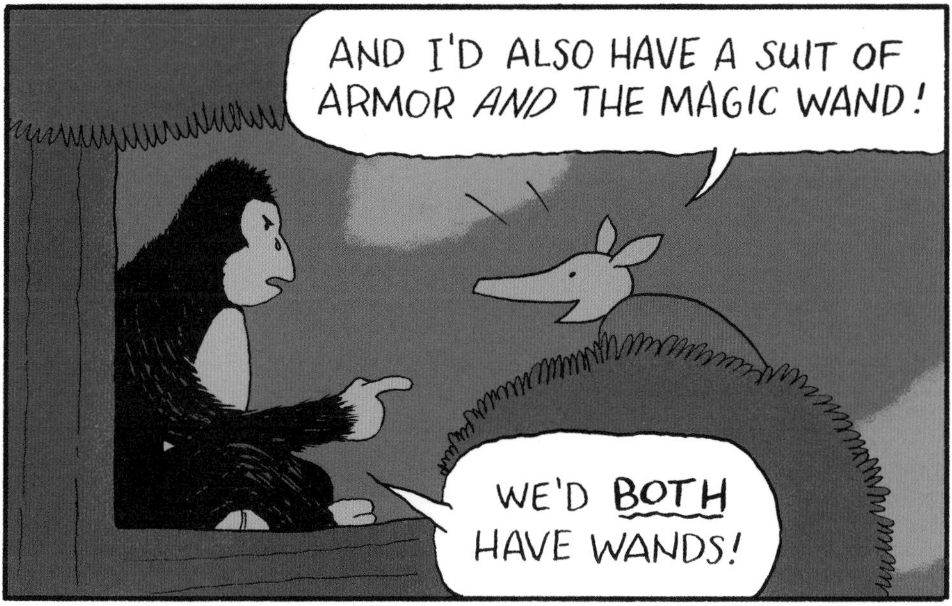
AND I'D ALSO HAVE A SUIT OF ARMOR *AND* THE MAGIC WAND!
WE'D **BOTH** HAVE WANDS!

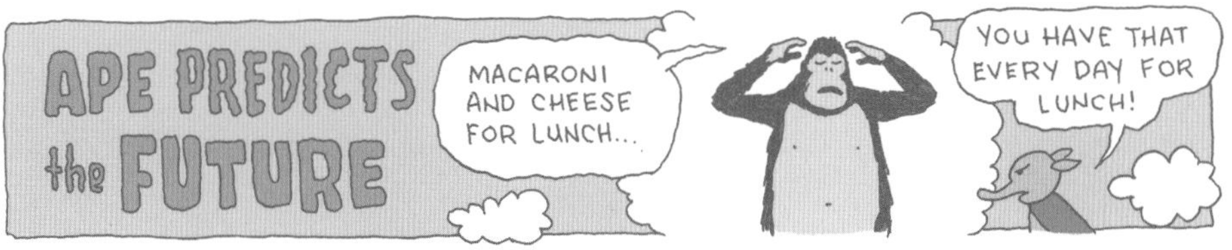
APE PREDICTS the FUTURE
MACARONI AND CHEESE FOR LUNCH...
YOU HAVE THAT EVERY DAY FOR LUNCH!

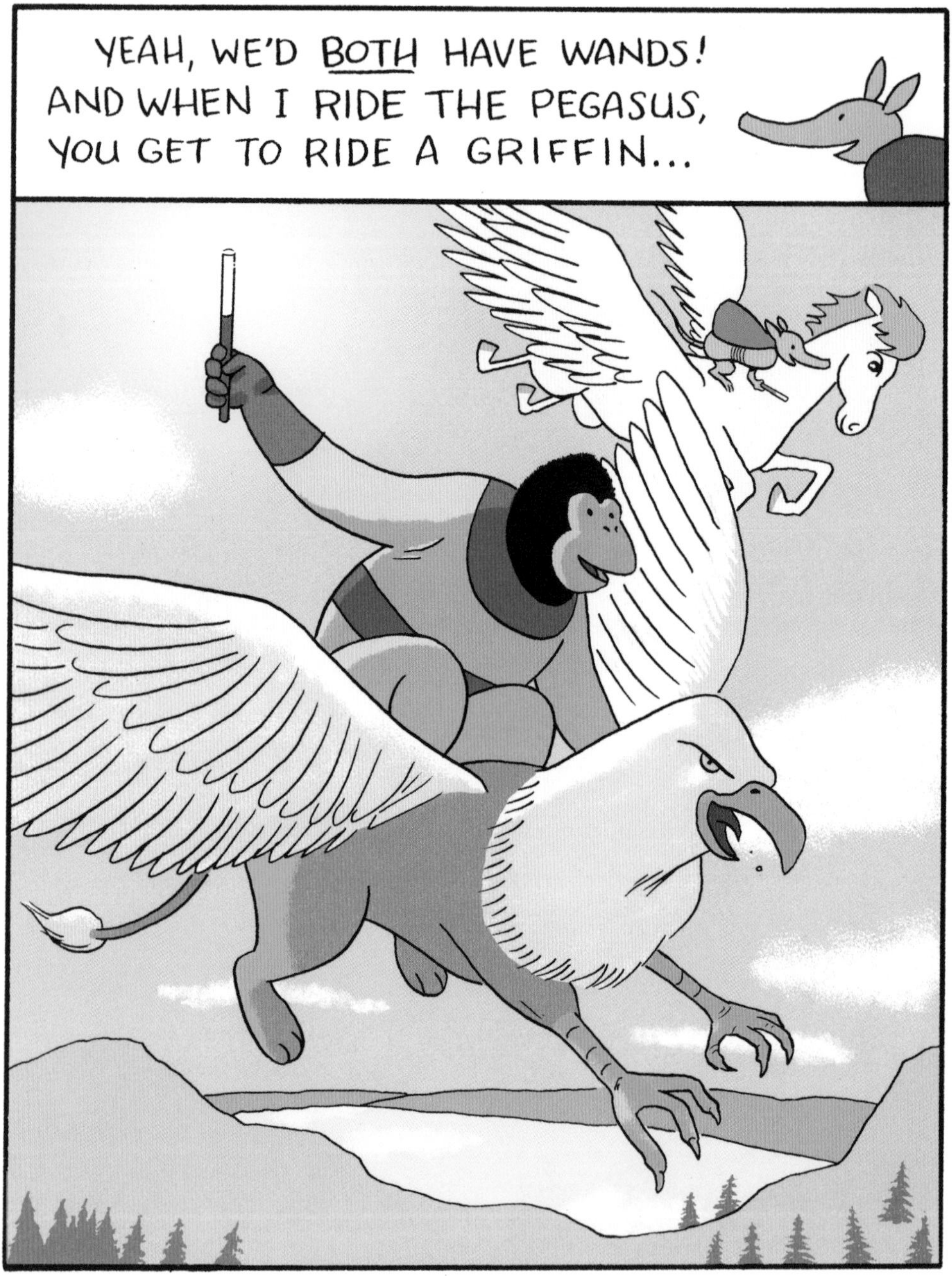
YEAH, WE'D BOTH HAVE WANDS! AND WHEN I RIDE THE PEGASUS, YOU GET TO RIDE A GRIFFIN...

OTHER THINGS APE DOES NOT LIKE

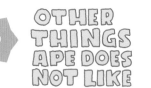

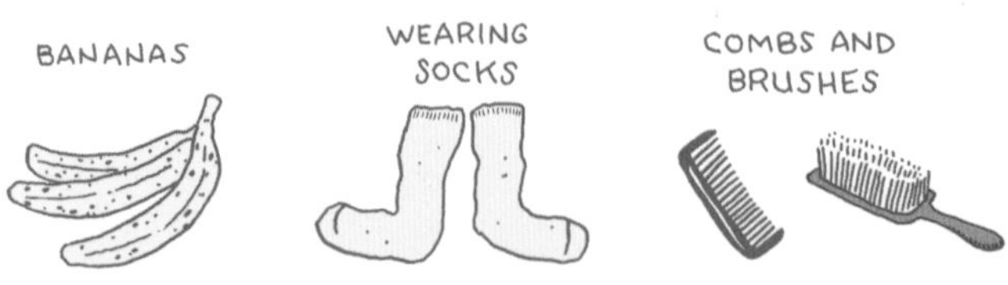
BANANAS
WEARING SOCKS
COMBS AND BRUSHES

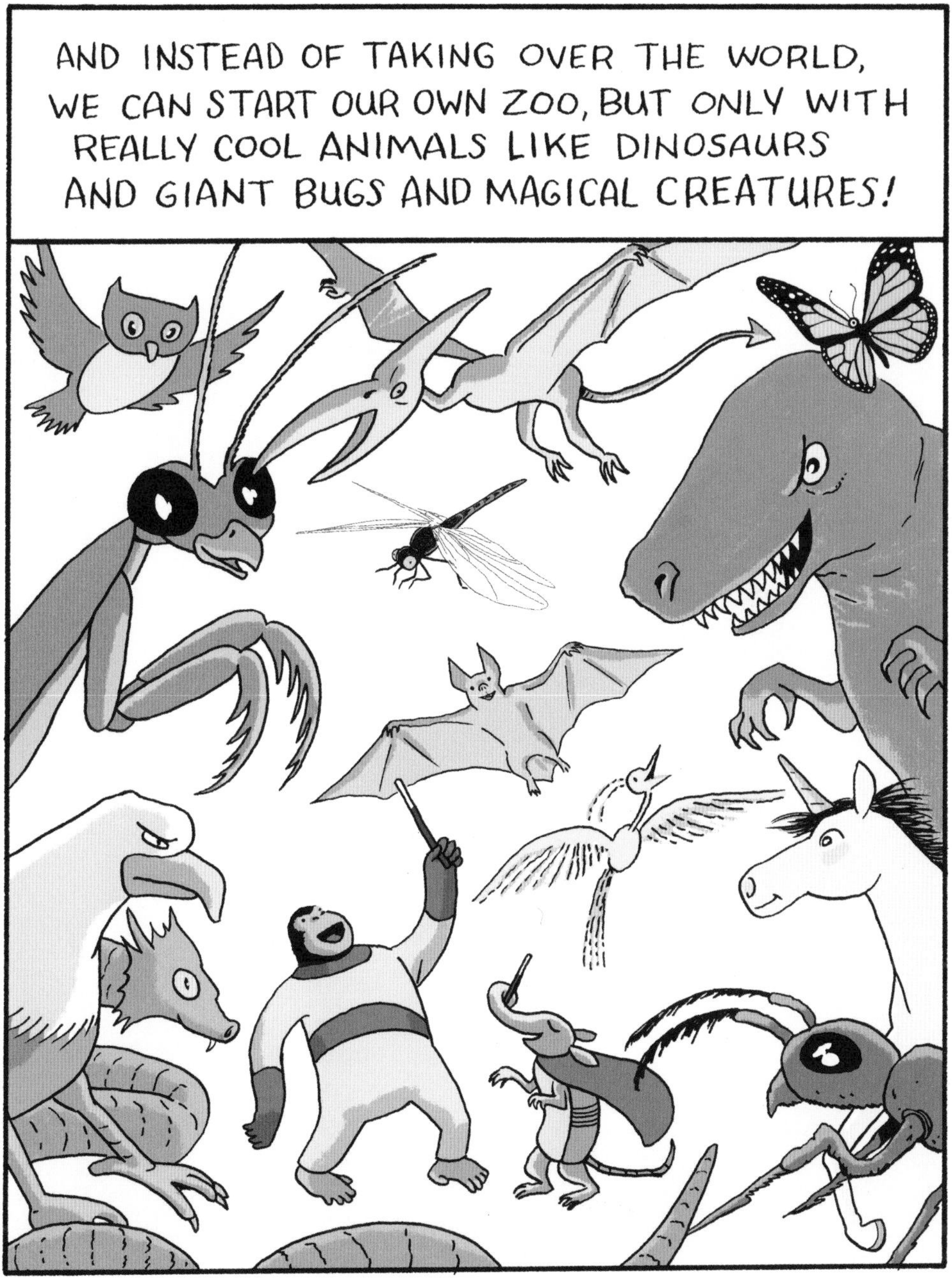
AND INSTEAD OF TAKING OVER THE WORLD, WE CAN START OUR OWN ZOO, BUT ONLY WITH REALLY COOL ANIMALS LIKE DINOSAURS AND GIANT BUGS AND MAGICAL CREATURES!

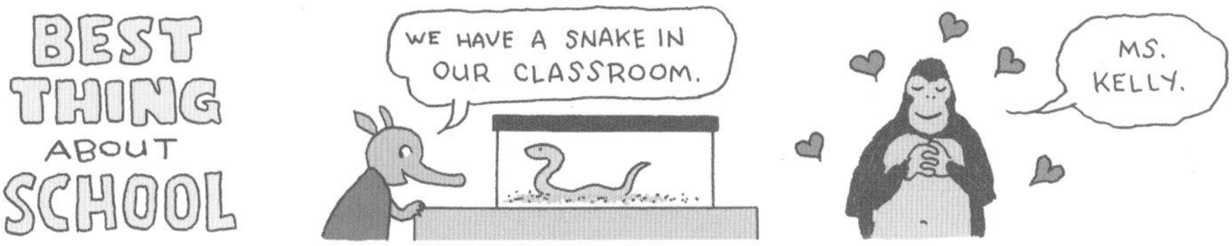
BEST THING ABOUT SCHOOL
WE HAVE A SNAKE IN OUR CLASSROOM.
MS. KELLY.

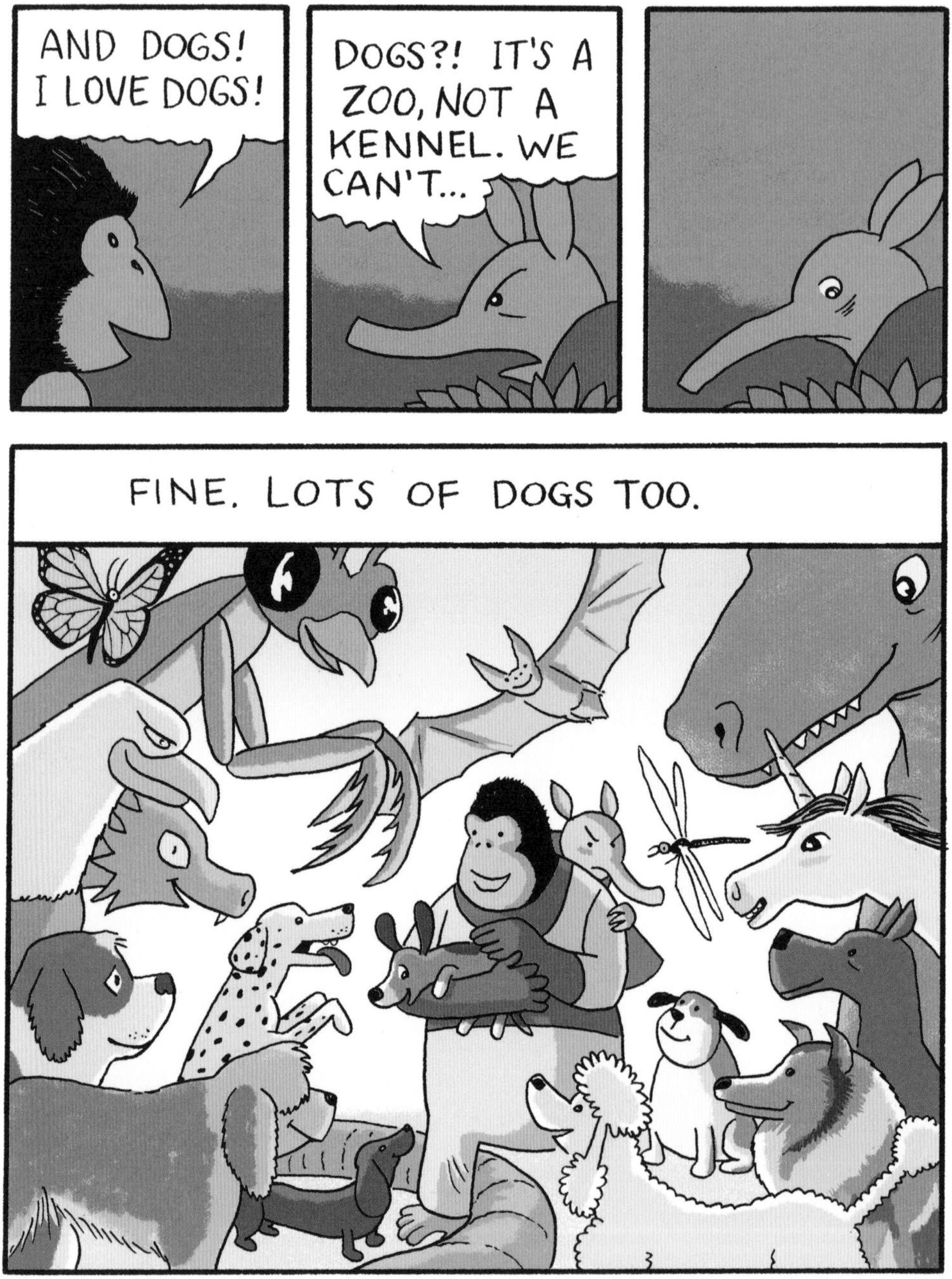
AND DOGS! I LOVE DOGS!
DOGS?! IT'S A ZOO, NOT A KENNEL. WE CAN'T...
FINE. LOTS OF DOGS TOO.

ARMADILLO'S FAVORITE CANDY

CARAMEL WITH CREAM IN THE MIDDLE

CANDY CORN

CARAMEL WITHOUT THE CREAM

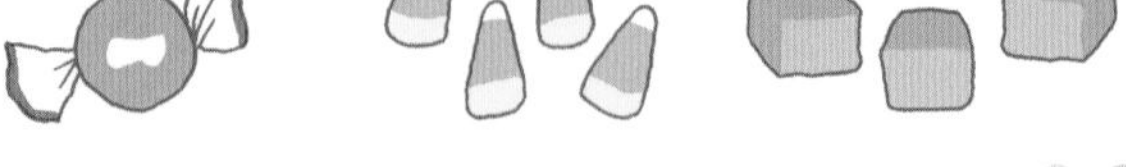

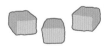

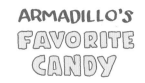

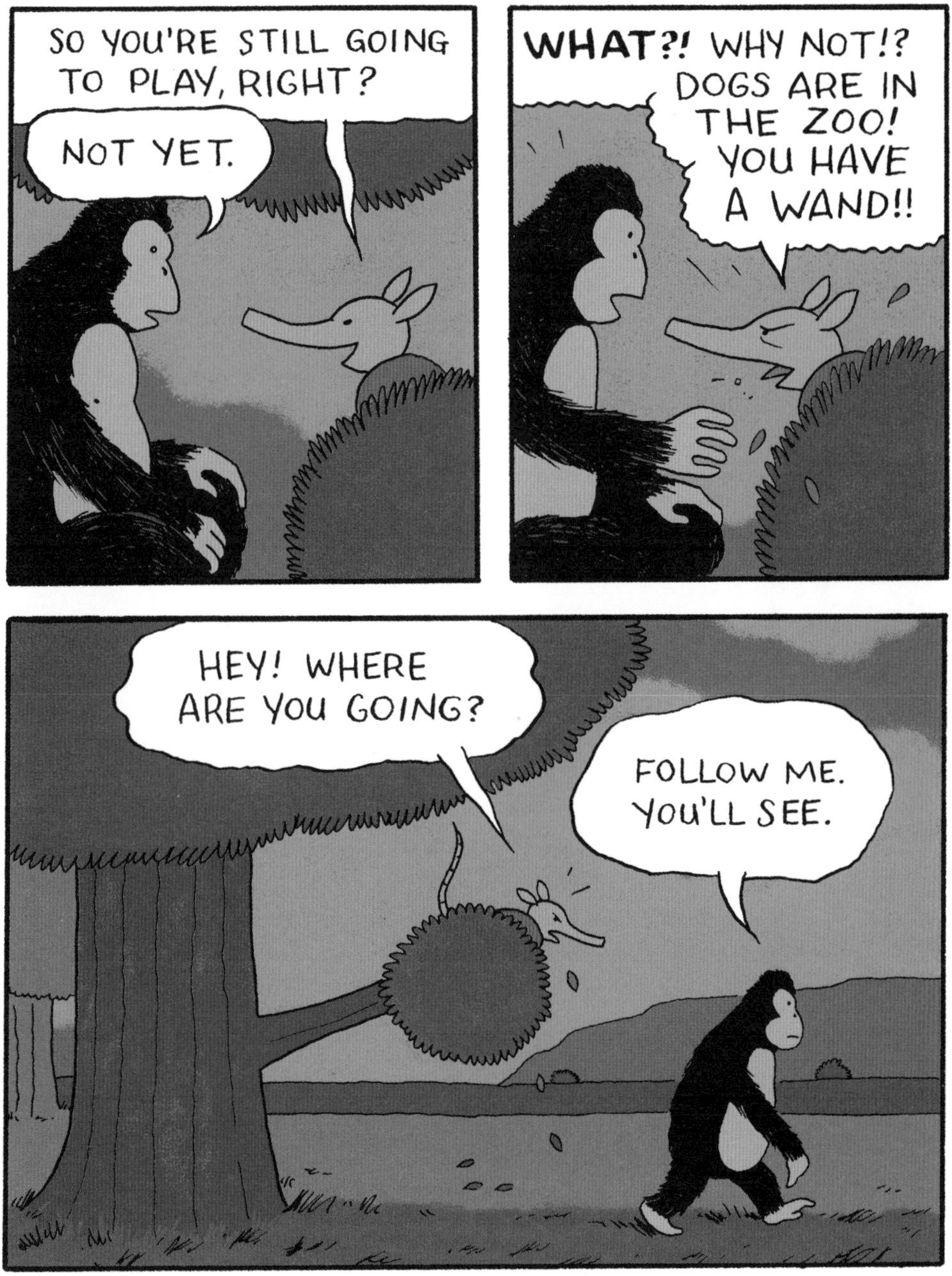
SO YOU'RE STILL GOING TO PLAY, RIGHT?
NOT YET.
WHAT?! WHY NOT!? DOGS ARE IN THE ZOO! YOU HAVE A WAND!!
HEY! WHERE ARE YOU GOING?
FOLLOW ME. YOU'LL SEE.

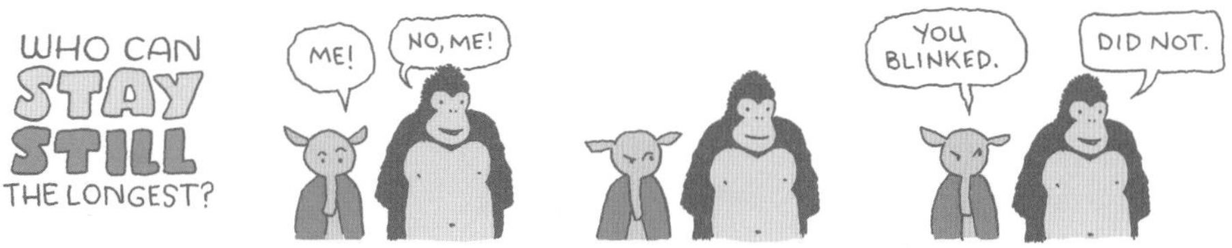
WHO CAN STAY STILL THE LONGEST?
ME!
NO, ME!
YOU BLINKED.
DID NOT.

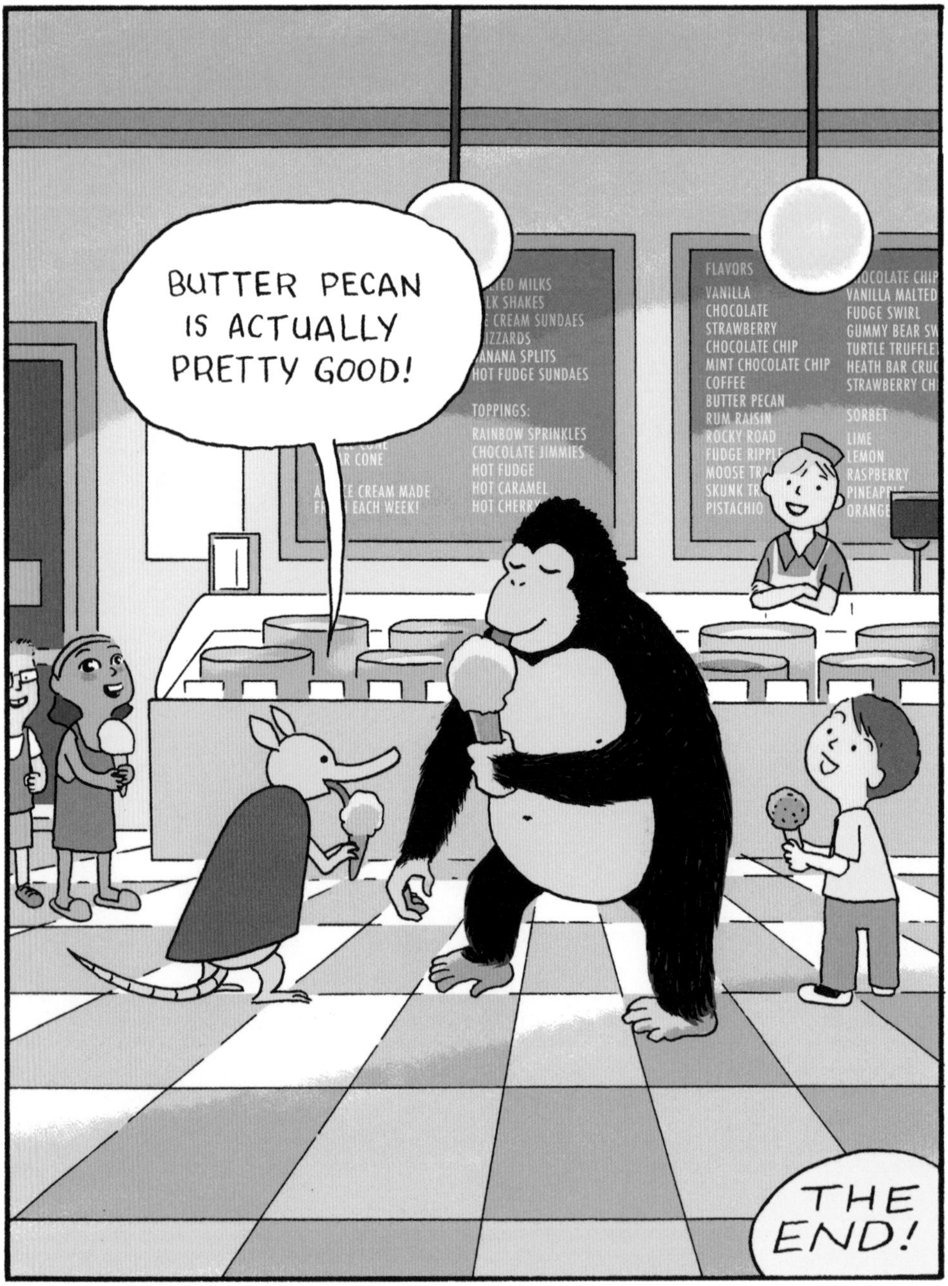
BUTTER PECAN IS ACTUALLY PRETTY GOOD!
HOT FUDGE SUNDAES
TOPPINGS:
RAINBOW SPRINKLES
CHOCOLATE JIMMIES
HOT FUDGE
HOT CARAMEL
FLAVORS
VANILLA
CHOCOLATE
STRAWBERRY
CHOCOLATE CHIP
MINT CHOCOLATE CHIP
COFFEE
BUTTER PECAN
RUM RAISIN
ROCKY ROAD
PISTACHIO
VANILLA MALTED
FUDGE SWIRL
SORBET
LIME
LEMON
RASPBERRY
THE END!

FINAL WORDS ?

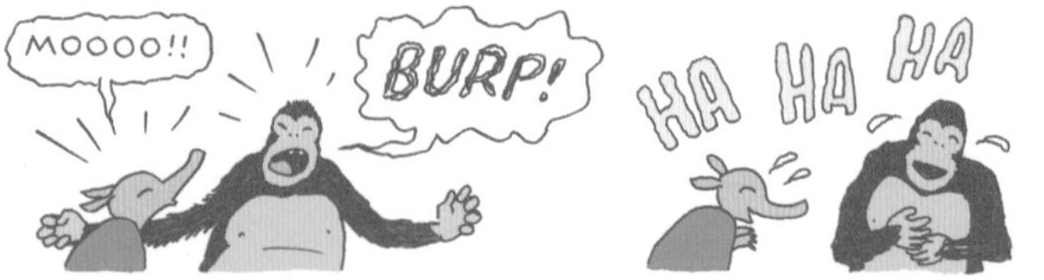
MOOOO!!
BURP!
HA HA HA

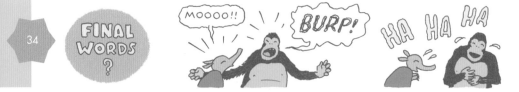

ABOUT THE AUTHOR

"One reason I make comics is to let my imagination run wild," says **JAMES STURM**, coauthor of the best-selling "Adventures in Cartooning" series and author of *Birdsong: A Story in Pictures,* a TOON Book. "I don't like people telling me what to draw, so I respect Armadillo for sticking to his vision. But what impresses me most is that Armadillo finds the strength to compromise when Ape's friendship is at stake."

Why an ape and an armadillo? "Visually, it's interesting to have one character who's really big and one who's much smaller–I went with these two because Elephant and Piggie were already taken."

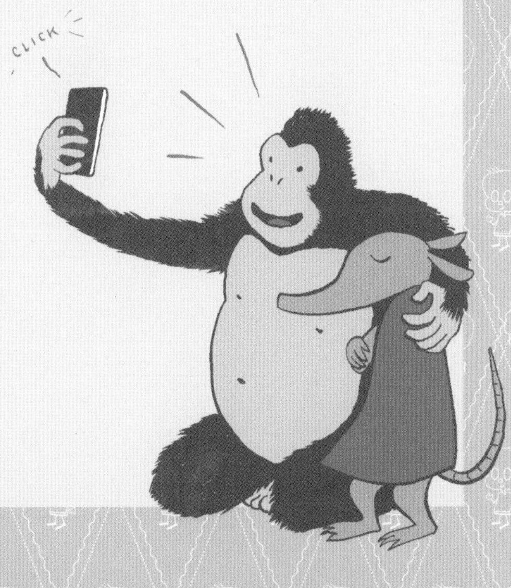
CLICK

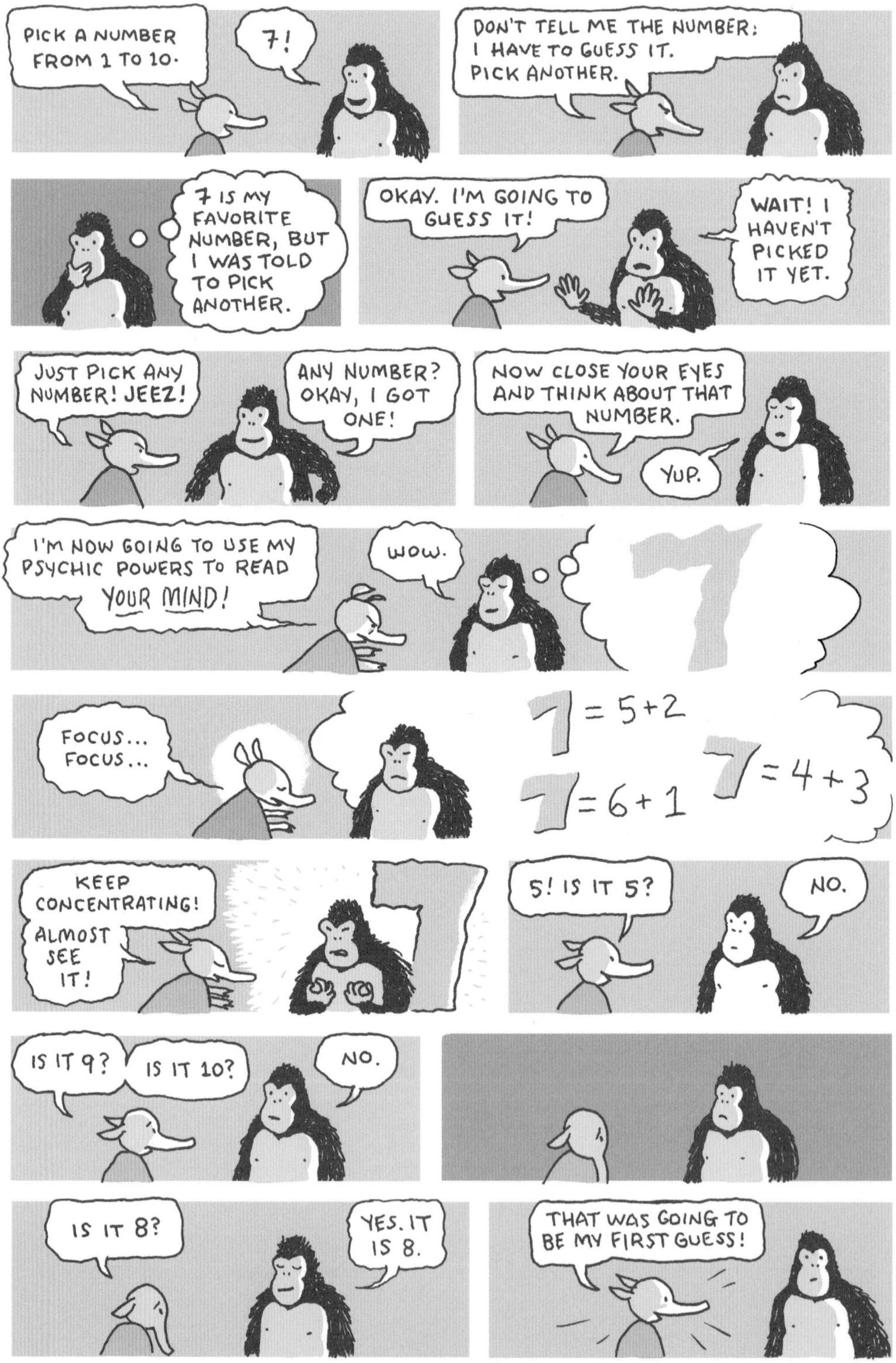
PICK A NUMBER FROM 1 TO 10.
7!
DON'T TELL ME THE NUMBER: I HAVE TO GUESS IT. PICK ANOTHER.
7 IS MY FAVORITE NUMBER, BUT I WAS TOLD TO PICK ANOTHER.
OKAY. I'M GOING TO GUESS IT!
WAIT! I HAVEN'T PICKED IT YET.
JUST PICK ANY NUMBER! JEEZ!
ANY NUMBER? OKAY, I GOT ONE!
NOW CLOSE YOUR EYES AND THINK ABOUT THAT NUMBER.
YUP.
I'M NOW GOING TO USE MY PSYCHIC POWERS TO READ YOUR MIND!
WOW.
7
FOCUS... FOCUS...
7 = 5+2
7 = 6+1
7 = 4+3
KEEP CONCENTRATING!
ALMOST SEE IT!
7
5! IS IT 5?
NO.
IS IT 9?
IS IT 10?
NO.
IS IT 8?
YES. IT IS 8.
THAT WAS GOING TO BE MY FIRST GUESS!

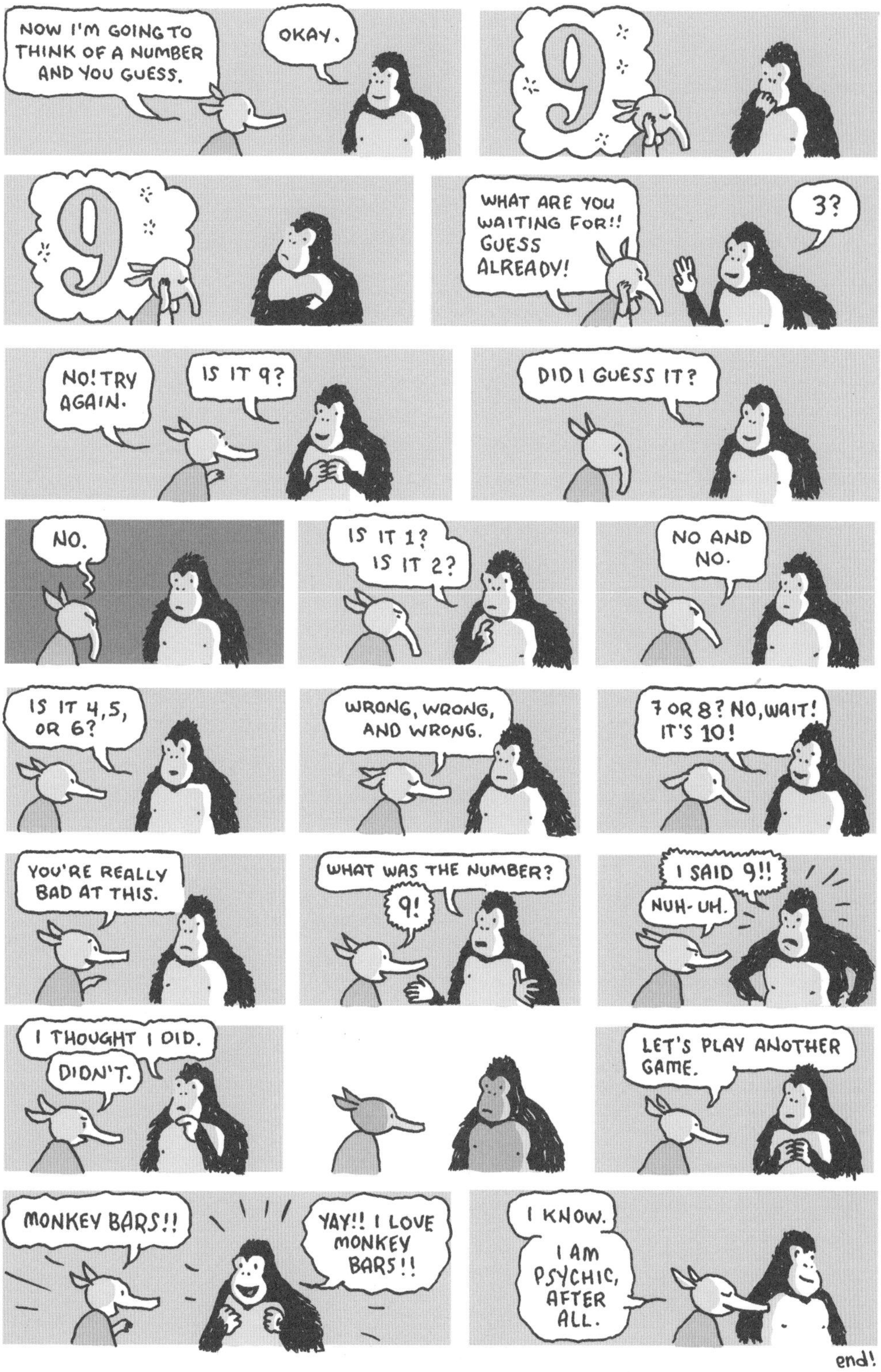
NOW I'M GOING TO THINK OF A NUMBER AND YOU GUESS.
OKAY.
9
9
WHAT ARE YOU WAITING FOR!! GUESS ALREADY!
3?
NO! TRY AGAIN.
IS IT 9?
DID I GUESS IT?
NO.
IS IT 1?
IS IT 2?
NO AND NO.
IS IT 4,5, OR 6?
WRONG, WRONG, AND WRONG.
7 OR 8? NO, WAIT! IT'S 10!
YOU'RE REALLY BAD AT THIS.
WHAT WAS THE NUMBER?
9!
I SAID 9!!
NUH-UH.
I THOUGHT I DID.
DIDN'T.
LET'S PLAY ANOTHER GAME.
MONKEY BARS!!
YAY!! I LOVE MONKEY BARS!!
I KNOW.
I AM PSYCHIC, AFTER ALL.
end!

HOW TO READ
COMICS WITH KIDS

Kids **love** comics! They are naturally drawn to the details in the pictures, which make them want to read the words. Comics beg for repeated readings and let both emerging and reluctant readers enjoy complex stories with a rich vocabulary. But since comics have their own grammar, here are a few tips for reading them with kids:

GUIDE YOUNG READERS: Use your finger to show your place in the text, but keep it at the bottom of the speaking character so it doesn't hide the very important facial expressions.

HAM IT UP! Think of the comic book story as a play, and don't hesitate to read with expression and intonation. Assign parts or get kids to supply the sound effects, a great way to reinforce phonics skills.

LET THEM GUESS. Comics provide lots of context for the words so emerging readers can make informed guesses. Like jigsaw puzzles, comics ask readers to make connections, so check a young audience's understanding by asking, "What's this character thinking?" (but don't be surprised if a kid finds some of the comics' subtle details faster than you).

TALK ABOUT THE PICTURES. Point out how the artist paces the story with pauses (silent panels) or speeded-up action (a burst of short panels). Discuss how the size and shape of the panels convey meaning.

ABOVE ALL, ENJOY! There is, of course, never one right way to read, so go for the shared pleasure. Once children make the story happen in their imagination, they have discovered the thrill of reading, and you won't be able to stop them. At that point, just go get them more books, and more comics.

TOON-BOOKS.com
SEE OUR FREE CARTOON MAKERS,
LESSON PLANS, AND MUCH MORE.